WHEN I FOUND YOU

KIRSTEN S. BLACKETER

DEDICATION

Ten years to write this, but it found the perfect moment.

To those who want to give up.

Don't.

You are loved beyond measure. <3

Table of Contents

CHAPTER ONE
KATHERINE

New Year's Eve, 2020

This year sucked. Every single brutal moment. I'm glad it's over, but a new year doesn't mean a fresh start. So, I took a walk to clear my head and ended up in the one place I could breathe. The place I associate with Dad, and now Mom. The loneliness intensifies as I stare out over the expanse of Lower Manhattan, an ominous twinkling maw of dark disappointment.

I embrace the howl of the wind whipping my hair. My eyes water and my cheeks and nose burn from the icy chill. I turn my back against it, snagging a perfect view of Freedom Tower gleaming in the distance.

I had to bribe the guard to give me ten minutes on the observation deck. My father worked in this building years ago. I can't see the Empire State Building without thinking of him. Or Mom. It seems only fitting to spend my final moments where I feel closest to them.

The past few months only added fuel to the raging dumpster fire that will forever be known as the year from hell. After the beginning of the year where a pandemic tipped the economic scales right into the toilet, I found myself unemployed as well as grieving. Not only did the six-year relationship with a man I thought I loved come to an abrupt end, but it happened only days after I lost Mom.

When this year started, I had hope, now I want nothing more than to join my parents in Brooklyn cemetery. Life is a joke, and I am no longer amused.

The city lay in eerie silence below. It should be raucous and vivacious celebrating the end of the shittiest year on record.

Instead, everyone hides inside their homes terrified of what the new year will bring.

A cold gust of air from the Hudson River and some scattered snow flakes wrap around me. I'm reminded of a film tucked somewhere in the back of my mind where two lovers meet on the top of the Empire State Building. But I'm not here to meet a lover. No, I'm here to end the miserable existence I call life.

This year took the very last fuck out of my savings account of fucks to give. I've got nothing left. Cancer took Mom in November. That was the final straw, honestly. While Mom was here, I had a purpose, a reason to keep going. Now, there's nothing. I can't even see a silver lining in the distance, it's all hazy and distorted like a mist hovering over the edge of a cliff. I might as well embrace the inevitable.

It's over.

I glance over the edge of the railing of the towering skyscraper. Since the lockdowns, the building management began construction on the observation deck, which removed the typical barriers protecting pedestrians from dealing with items being tossed from a hundred floors up. But now there's nothing between me and the ledge. The lights of Freedom Tower flicker in the distance. A beacon of hope and perseverance, but I remember, and it does nothing to quell the hopelessness constricting my heart.

I lean over the rail. A gust of wind pushes against my back giving me the nudge I need. Reflexively, I grip the rail tighter. If I die, it'll be on my terms, damn it. I won't let fate take this from me too.

The once great, thriving city that never sleeps slumbers beneath my feet. I close my eyes and pray. I ask for forgiveness, for some semblance of clarity. Something. Anything.

My phone rings and one hand slips from the railing. I flounder for a moment, and my heart lodges in my throat. I grip the railing with one hand, my back to the world below until the ringing stops. Carefully, I remove my phone from my pocket.

Unknown caller.

Figures. I swipe up to unlock my phone. A gust of wind blows across the deck. I stumble back, but the phone slips from my grip and falls. I watch in slow motion as my phone tumbles through the air and drops toward to the street below.

It's a sign. It has to be. I take a deep breath. Maybe this isn't the solution. Maybe I should give the new year a chance. How could things possibly get any worse?

"Hey, lady. What the hell are you doing?" A beam of light shines right in my eye.

My heart pounds in my throat. I jump and my hand slips, making me twist around in a blur. The whole world sinks into slow motion, just like my phone, as I fall back into the open space surrounding the Empire State Building. A scream tears from my throat as I grab for the railing, but it's too late. It's over. I'm falling.

I watch the beam of light grow smaller and smaller until it's a pinprick in the distance. The lights of the Empire State Building create a halo overhead as I fall. This is better, falling backward. That way I don't see what's coming.

My mind accepts the inevitable. I'm on my way, Mom. Dad, I'll see you soon. I stare into the heavens as I drift through the cold air, but surprisingly, I'm no longer cold. What a way to celebrate New Year's Eve. Is it midnight yet? Does it matter?

Not anymore. I close my eyes and embrace the inevitable.

The impact I expected never comes. I wait for a moment, and it stretches into several moments. Did I survive the fall? No, this can't be right.

I crack open one eye.

The sun rises over the bay casting the city in beautiful shades of red and orange. Huh? Maybe I imagined falling. I grip the railing and whip my head around in disbelief.

The observation deck is empty except for me. I check my pockets. Nope, my phone is definitely gone. I inhale deeply wondering if I somehow passed out last night and woke up from the nightmare which seemed so damn real.

The skyline spreads before me like a panoramic photograph. It's gorgeous. Wait.

I blink twice before it hits me like a dump truck on the Washington Bridge.

"No, it can't be." I mutter before rubbing my eyes and looking again. But the scenery doesn't change.

It's the skyline I've known my whole life, but there's something wrong. Instead of Freedom Tower, there are two identical towers stretching into the sky on the southern tip of Manhattan Island. The Twin Towers. The ones that fell on September 11th, 2001.

"No. They're not there." I turn and face the building. After several deep breaths, I spin around and take in the view once more.

They're still there. The World Trade Center Towers stand tall against the sunrise.

I back up until I hit the wall. No, what's going on? This can't be right.

A garbage can in the corner catches my eye. There's a newspaper tucked behind it. I rush over and pull it out.

Spreading it on the ground, I scan the headlines and search for the date. December 31, 1984. I read it over and over hoping it's a joke, a prank. Someone's mad at me for trying to kill myself, so they've decided to pull a fast one on me, show me how lucky I am or something stupid.

I stand up and spin around. No one. Nothing. No cameras, no phones recording my reaction. Not a goddamn thing. What the fuck?

I snatch up the paper and tuck it under my arm. There has to be a reasonable explanation for this. There has to be. I chew on my lip and run through the possibilities in my mind.

Damn. I've got nothing. The paper crumples under my arm. Okay, I need a minute.

One more peek to confirm I'm not insane. Nope. The towers are still there. I take three deep breaths focusing all my energy on filling my lungs with air. The cold stone beneath my fingertips grounds me. After several minutes, a calm settles over me.

I open my eyes and find the sun rising in the distance. The

towers cast shadows over the city below. If I'm actually in the year 1985, then I haven't been born yet. My birthday isn't until June. Shit. Mom is pregnant with me right now.

What the hell is happening? I take another deep breath and focus on the facts I have. Where did we live when I was born? Dad. Holy shit. Dad.

Excitement bubbles up from the pit of my stomach. Dad's alive. Tears fill my eyes. I can see Dad again. I cry out in relief.

Wait. Remember. What did Mom tell me?

Dad died when I was three years old. February 17, 1989. That's more than enough time to find him. Where did she say he worked?

It hits me like a slap to the face. The Empire State Building. It's why I came here in the first place. To find a connection to Dad. To have him talk me out of this insanity. In some strange way I wanted him to reach out and stop me, to give me some hope for the future. Is it possible he had a hand in this?

I shake my head. No. This is insane. All of it. I didn't try to kill myself. I didn't end up traveling through time. This isn't 1985. I'm dead. This isn't real.

"Ma'am?" a voice echoes across the small observation deck.

I jump and spin around to face the voice intruding on my existential moment with the universe. "Yes, sorry."

"Ma'am, what are you doing up here? The deck doesn't open for another two hours."

"Oh." I laugh and wave a hand. "It's a long story. I'll go." As I head for the elevator, the man follows behind me.

"Are you okay, ma'am?" he asks as the doors close sealing us inside the elevator car.

"Yes, of course." I clear my throat. "Why do you ask?"

"If you don't mind my being blunt, ma'am, you don't look well." He pressed the button for the ground floor.

A memory flashes in my mind. The number fifty-four. I grasp it with both hands. "Would you mind pressing floor fifty-four? I forgot something."

He eyes me suspiciously. I force a smile, and he shrugs before pressing the button I requested. When it stops, he turns to face me.

"I'll be on the ground floor. Let me know if you need help with anything."

The doors slide open. Nervous excitement churns in my gut. "Thank you. I will."

I step into the hallway and turn to the left, unsure of which direction I should go but knowing I need to put some distance between me and the man who found me on the rooftop.

The elevator doors close and the numbers start declining on the illuminated panel over the elevator. I breathe easier.

It's early. No one is in any of the offices yet. Right? I locate the information board and scan the list of offices on this floor.

Lawyers. Bankers. There it is. Lincoln Architecture Firm. Beneath it, I read the list of employees barely registering the names until one douses me with ice water. *Jackpot.*

I rest my hand on the name. Mr. Victor Cohen. *Dad.* I close my eyes and breathe deep.

Is this really happening? Shit. It's New Year's Day. If it wasn't a holiday, he would be arriving for work shortly. I glance around the deserted floor and spy their main office door. I try it, but it's locked. Damn.

I could wait here until he shows up. No. That could be days. I haven't showered, and there's nothing to eat. My stomach rumbles at the thought.

Then a stray thought built from years of watching science fiction paralyzes me. What if I screw up some space time continuum or create a paradox by seeing him? But nothing's proven. It's all theoretical. I mean, everything will be fine, right?

Besides, I think a paradox only happens when you encounter yourself, and I haven't even been born yet since my birthday isn't until June. I clap my hand over my mouth and stifle a chuckle. Holy hell, this is freaky. If this is New Year's Day 1985, then Mom is in her mid-twenties and Dad's just hit thirty. I'm older than my parents now.

But they're alive. A small voice whispers. Hope blossoms in my chest. I can see them again, then reality hits me with a baseball bat. They don't know me, and they'll think I'm crazy if

I tell them who I am.

It doesn't matter. It's Dad. Nothing can stop me from seeing him. Not a goddamn thing.

I need a plan.

My foot crunches on a piece of paper as I step away from the door. I retrieve it, noting the name at the top of the page. *Mr. Arthur Maxwell.*

A noise behind the office door startles me, but before I can react, the door swings open. A shooting pain thunders through my head and over my shoulders. The world goes dark.

CHAPTER TWO
ARTHUR

The door meeting resistance should have worried me, but it didn't. This wasn't the first time some idiot put a chair or trash bin in front of the office entrance. For an architecture firm, the floor layout was as unfortunate as the door placement since it aligned perfectly with the elevator doors creating all types of traffic issues during the workday. I shove the door open with my shoulder, and it slams into something.

I peer around the edge of the door and frown. There's no one there. Then I glance down at the floor and my blood turns to ice. Shit. A dark-haired woman wearing winter boots and an oversized wool coat lay sprawled at my feet. Is she breathing?

Tossing aside my briefcase, I kneel beside her and feel for a pulse. Okay, she's alive at least. I roll her onto her back with little resistance. Her pale skin reflects a hint of color, and she's breathing steadily, as though trapped in a deep sleep. Her thick eyelashes lay heavy against her cheeks.

She looks familiar. Maybe one of the maids working overtime on the holiday? I brush my hand across her forehead, removing the dark waves when I notice the smear of blood across her hairline.

"Fuck." I gently rock her. "Ma'am. Can you hear me? Ma'am? Goddamn it, wake up." My prodding does nothing, and there's no way to hide the panic rising in my voice.

I can't call the cops or an ambulance. The last thing I need right now is an investigation into why this woman is lying on the floor outside my office with a headwound. I know enough lawyers to know involving the cops is a one-way ticket to trouble. With the upcoming proposal meeting with the Hudson Group for a new hotel in Manhattan around the corner, I can't take any chances of having an incident, no matter how accidental, ruin such a prime opportunity.

I sound like a heartless bastard. With a groan I place my briefcase inside the office and lock the door. The woman doesn't even whimper when I pull her into my arms and shift her body against me. I stumble a bit under the weight but quickly find a comfortable position. I'm too old for this shit.

I press the down button next to the elevator. When the car arrives, I step in and select the ground floor. Her head rests against my shoulder lolling from the elevator's wobbly descent. My driver should still be waiting outside. I only meant to come into the office for a moment and verify some paperwork. Then she happened. I glance down at the woman in my arms and squash the protective instinct rising from the pit of my subconscious.

No. You're not her knight in shining armor. You knocked her out. Now you're kidnapping her. What kind of man are you, Arthur? If I could reach inside my own mind and rip out the part of my brain now accosting me, I would do it without hesitation. Instead, I ignore it and focus on the numbers as they count down.

When we reach the ground floor, the guard's eyes widen when I step from the elevator carrying the unconscious woman.

"Mr. Maxwell." He rushes forward. "What happened, sir?"

"Oh, one of my new temp secretaries. She fell asleep in the lounge late last night, and I can't seem to wake her." I shrug but it's lost under her weight pressed against my chest.

The guard doesn't seem too convinced with my lie, but he doesn't need to believe me. One of the regular guards appears around the corner. Mike. He's worked at the building since I started here fifteen years ago.

"Oh, I see you found her." Mike gestures to the woman in my arms. "She was up on the observation deck this morning. Asked me to stop on your floor. She one of your employees?"

I nod. "Yes, started last week. A temp."

"She looked a little lost up there on the deck this morning." He stuffs his hands in his pockets. "Might want to keep an eye on her."

"Yeah. Found her passed out on the couch in the lounge. I guess the party was too much for her." I tsk. "Well, gents. I need to get her home."

"No problem, Mr. Maxwell. Happy New Year." Mike tips his head and motions for the other guard to open the door.

Once I step out into the cold morning air, I exhale with relief. The black Cadillac pulls up to the curb ahead. When my driver, Cyril, steps around the car, his brow arches in surprise. He says nothing and opens the rear door.

It takes a bit of fancy maneuvering, but I manage to get her comfortably situated in the back seat and slide in next to her. She's still unconscious. I sigh. What a way to start the new year.

Cyril slides into the driver's seat and glances at me in the rearview. "Where to, sir?"

"Home." I catch the glimmer of curiosity and open criticism in his eyes.

"Yes, sir." He pulls away from the curb and out into the early traffic.

I pinch the bridge of my nose and take a deep breath. What the hell am I going to do with this mess? I peek at the woman beside me. A pronounced smear of blood mars her forehead. I'm a horrible person. I should have called for help or at least let her rest in the office until she woke up. But no. I didn't need this kind of gossip spreading through the office, let alone the building.

Within fifteen minutes, I'm inside the penthouse elevator with the mysterious woman limp in my arms. It takes some time to slide the key in the lock, but once we're inside the apartment, a weight lifts from my shoulders. I carry her to my bed and lay her on the down coverlet.

She moans and shifts but doesn't wake. I unbutton her coat and slip it from her shoulders. The oversized monstrosity hinders me from assessing whether or not I did more damage than a knock on the head. I set it aside, noting the familiar designer style much like the new coat Victor bought last month, but the material is worn and well-loved. I shove the thought aside. A puzzle to ponder later.

After a quick inspection, I note no other injuries with a sigh of relief. I gather towels, a wet cloth, and the first aid kit I keep for emergencies.

Her lashes flutter when I brush the cloth over her hairline. The blood washes easily enough from her dark hair, but the raised bump above her hairline bleeds afresh when I dab it. A cut, not too deep, but enough to cause a deceptive amount of visual trauma. I must have caught her with the edge of the door.

Guilt washes over me. Maybe I should have taken her to the hospital. At least then I could be assured of her care, even if the circumstances of her injury seem suspicious. I take a breath and head into the kitchen to get something cold to compress over the wound.

I grab the phone and dial the number I know by heart.

"Dr. Thompson."

"Hey, it's Arthur."

"Hey. You're up early. Didn't you have a party at the office last night?"

I rake my hand through my hair wishing I had cut it last week. "Yeah, but we went home shortly after midnight. Are you on call today?"

"No." Rob pauses. *"Do you need something or are you calling to wish me a Happy New Year?"*

"Can you come over? I need your help with something."

"Did you murder someone and you need me to help hide the body?" Rob chuckles. *"That shit will cost you. We're not kids anymore, you know. I have ethics I'm bound to."*

"Exactly, which is why I need you to get your ass over here." I groan. "Bring your bag of miracles."

"What happened?" The tone of Rob's voice shifts, and I can tell he's worried.

"I'll explain when you get here." I hang up the phone before he has a chance to respond. He'll keep me on the line all day if I let him. Hopefully it's enough of a teaser to convince him to come over.

When I return to the unconscious woman in my bed, I place the bag of frozen peas in a towel and place it on the lump. Then

I pull a blanket up over her. A soft moan makes me pause. She twitches her nose and exhales.

My gaze drifts over her features. Delicate brows, full lips, and a nose curved slightly off center. I wonder what color her eyes are. Probably a bewitching shade of brown or vibrant blue. The thought swiftly fixes itself in my mind and I'm thrown off.

I don't know anything about this woman. I've already dug myself into a nest of lies and perjured myself for her. I push aside any idle curiosity I have for her and focus instead on at least establishing an identity.

Carefully, I peel back the blanket to check her pockets. Wait, no pockets. What kind of garments are these? Some form of exercise leggings I expect, only made from thick material to provide warmth. The oversized cream sweater hides her figure. I search her innocently, ignoring her soft curves. *No pockets and no identification.* I frown. The overcoat.

I pick it up from the chair and search every pocket. A handful of crumpled papers, a key, and a stick of gum wrapped tight in silver paper. Great. Nothing.

The doorbell startles me. I dash across the apartment and open the door.

Rob steps inside carrying a small leather case. "What the hell is going on?"

I lock the door and lead him into my bedroom, gesturing to the woman lying in my bed as though it were a grand revelation and would explain itself.

"What the fuck did you do?" Rob rushes to her side and checks her pulse. He's quick and thorough. I watch him follow the same methodical procedures he learned when he was in med school.

"I went to the office this morning to get some paperwork I forgot. When I went to leave, I hit her with the door." I lift my hands in supplication when Rob turns and shakes his head. "By accident. It was a fucking accident, okay?"

He returns his attention to the woman. "How long has she been unconscious?"

I shrug. "I don't know. An hour maybe?"

"An hour?" Rob grits his teeth. "You should've called me right away."

"Why?" Fear grips me and I know I'm going to hell for not calling the ambulance. "Is it bad?"

Rob peels back the makeshift ice pack and inspects the wound on her head. He tuts and replaces the cold pack. "No. But I don't like the fact she hasn't regained consciousness."

I stand steadfast in my decision as he takes her pulse and checks the dilation of her eyes.

"What's her name?" He reaches into his bag.

"I don't know. I've never seen her in the building before."

"Does she have any identification? A driver's license?" He fishes around searching for something in the bottom of the bag.

"No." I cross my arms, bracing against the judgement emanating off Rob in waves. If we weren't friends for the last twenty-odd years, I would tell him exactly where to take his sorry ass. Truth is, I need his help, and he knows it.

He opens a small case and withdraws an ammonia capsule. I catch a brief hint of it when he cracks it open and waves it under her nose.

She jolts against the assault of chemicals. Her eyes fly open, not blue. Not brown. A mixture of the two. *Interesting.* Wild, she lurches upright and grips her head with a tentative hand, hissing as her fingertips brush the abrasion.

"Take it easy. You're safe." Rob sits on the edge of the bed and smiles. I want to slap him already. His bedside manner always earns him bonus points at the hospital. I stay back and observe from the side.

"Where am I?" She blinks, trying to remember but obviously struggling. "Who are you?"

"I'm Rob. This is Arthur. You're in his apartment. You are injured. Do you remember what happened?" Rob's soothing voice seems to work its magic as she relaxes her shoulders.

She licks her lips and scrunches her nose in thought. "I was at the Empire State Building..." She mutters almost to herself. Her eyes widen. "Am I dead?"

Rob chuckles. "No, most certainly not dead."

Her gaze drifts to the window overlooking the southern tip of Manhattan. I chose this apartment for the skyline view of the most iconic skyscrapers in the world. It cost me a fortune, but it was worth every penny.

When her gaze fixes on me, her enchanting eyes are wide with terror. I want to reach out and comfort her, but I stand my ground, watching and waiting.

Rob takes her hand. "What's your name, sweetheart?"

"Katherine." She turns to face him. "But everyone calls me Kate."

"Okay, Kate. You rest here for a minute. I'll get something to replenish your fluids. Stay in bed, okay?" Rob stands and motions for me to join him.

With one last look at the lost soul in my bed, I follow Rob into the living room and brace myself for the lecture of the century. At least she's okay. *Kate.* What the hell have I gotten myself into now?

CHAPTER THREE
KATHERINE

A rancid smell rips me from the tormented dreams. The moment I open my eyes pain shoots through my head. Holy shit. Am I dead? In a slow-motion delayed reaction, I realize I'm no longer at the Empire State Building. I'm in a bed in a fancy apartment, and I'm not alone.

The man hovering beside the bed has dark blonde hair, cropped close in a military-esque style, but professional with a length that makes him approachable. His soft hazel eyes scan my face and he smiles. He sits on the edge of the bed.

"Take it easy. You're safe."

"Where am I?" I struggle with the words. My tongue feels thick and my head aches so much I can barely think. "Who are you?"

"I'm Rob. This is Arthur." He gestures to the man behind him standing at the foot of the bed.

I'm struck stupid at the sight of Arthur. He's tall with dark brown hair, nearly black. His steel gray eyes pin me with unyielding curiosity. There's nothing soft about his expression or his features. He looks carved from marble, like he belongs in a museum alongside David, not here painted in warm hues and vibrant colors.

"You're in his apartment." Rob continues, his voice soothing and calm, "You were injured. Do you remember what happened?"

It takes me a minute to remember. "I was at the Empire State Building…" Oh, shit. Maybe I did jump. "Am I dead?"

Rob chuckles. "No, most certainly not dead."

I relax only a fraction until I glance out the window. The southern tip of Manhattan lays on the horizon with the Empire

State Building standing tall against the blue sky, then I see the World Trade Center buildings. The Twin Towers. Holy shit, it wasn't a dream. I really did travel through time.

The memories flash through my mind. My phone dropping off the top of the building. When I slipped. The guard finding me. The elevator. The realization. Dad and Mom. They're alive. His office. The paper. Shit, the door.

I meet Arthur's gaze and his jaw ticks almost imperceptibly. Oh, lord. Am I in trouble? What the hell happened?

It barely registers when Rob takes my hand. "What's your name, sweetheart?"

"Katherine." I meet his warm, friendly gaze. They don't need my full name, right? I left my ID in my purse, and who knows where the hell it is now. "But everyone calls me Kate."

"Okay, Kate. You rest here for a minute. I'll get something to replenish your fluids. Stay in bed, okay?" Rob rises to his feet and motions for Arthur to follow him.

I'm relieved, because being in the same room with that man brought a wave of awareness I wasn't quite ready to examine yet. When the door closes, I slowly rise to my feet and cross the room to crack it open hoping they don't notice. I peek into the room ignoring the thundering headache pounding through my skull. Both men stand in the kitchen, their backs to the bedroom where they left me.

"What the hell did you do, Arthur?" Rob keeps his voice low and rips open the refrigerator.

What did he do? I rub the extremely tender lump on my head and wince when my hand brushes the cut and comes away damp with blood. I remember standing outside the office and leaning down to pick up a paper, then shooting pain and darkness.

"It was a fucking accident, Rob." He rakes his hand through his hair making it stand on end. "What should I have done? Huh? Called the cops. Rushed her to the hospital in an ambulance. Made a scene."

His restless discomfort makes me pause. It was an accident. For all I knew, I was alone on the fifty-fourth floor. My body sways and I brace myself against the doorway determined to hear what they're discussing about me.

"You should have called me. I could have met you at the office." The handsome doctor sets the orange juice container down on the counter with little grace.

"I know. Okay? I fucked up. Is that what you want me to admit? I panicked and made a stupid ass decision. There's nothing I can do about it now."

Rob pours some orange juice into a glass and replaces the cap on the jug. "Do you recognize her? From the building?"

Arthur shakes his head. "No. I mean she seems familiar, but hell, there are so many offices in the building and so much foot traffic. She could be any one of a hundred faces I pass every day."

Familiar, huh? I nearly laugh at the absurdity of the whole situation. There's no way in hell anyone in this time would recognize me. Mom always told me I looked like Dad, but I never quite saw the resemblance in the photographs she showed me over the years.

"You're going to keep an eye on her, right?" Rob asks with a pointed glance at his companion, whose grim expression casts a dark thundercloud over his head.

"Yeah," Arthur snaps. "I'm not a heartless bastard."

The duo moves back toward the bedroom and I jump away from the door hurrying back to the bed in time to collapse against the soft bedding as the door opens. My head pounds. I press my palm to my forehead and hiss in a breath.

Rob enters the room first bearing a glass of orange juice. He sets it on the nightstand and helps me sit up.

"Take it easy." His voice is soothing and calm. "I don't need you passing out. Here." He offers the orange juice and turns back to dig through the bag he brought. "Take these too."

I take the two pills from his palm and pop them in my mouth, washing them down with a few sips of juice. The sweet tart of the liquid tingles on my tongue. I drink the rest down quickly and sigh before handing him the glass.

My gaze drifts from the deep calm pools of Rob's hazel eyes to the tumultuous maelstrom raging in Arthur's, who stands at the foot of the bed with his arms folded across his chest. I can't tell if he's watching us with avid attention or barely restrained irritation.

I turn my gaze to the window overlooking the city. The sunset reflects off the buildings creating an illuminated maze weaving through the streets below with skyscrapers jutting up from the concrete jungle.

"Kate." Rob's soft but assertive voice pulls me from the view. When I face him, he smiles. "Is there anyone we can call? Family? Friends? Your husband, maybe?"

I shake my head. Hopelessness threatens to choke me. "Not married." I show my bare fingers. Scrambling for excuses I lunge for the most cliché of them all and it's enough to make me cringe. "But honestly, my head is a blur. I can't remember."

"Amnesia isn't uncommon after a head injury." Rob nods solemnly. "A few days of rest should help." He turns to his friend. "Can she stay for a few days, see if her memory comes back?" At Arthur's nod, he turns his attention back to me. "I'll make some inquiries at the hospital to see if anyone's been searching for you."

Unable to trust my ability to lie, I smile. "Thank you."

"I'll check on you tomorrow." He slowly rises to his feet and closes his bag. "Stay in bed. Rest. No sudden movements and no alcohol. Doctor's orders." His lopsided grin is so endearing it makes me forget I'm in the wrong decade if only for a moment.

"Yes, sir." I return his easy banter but my smile disappears the moment I see Arthur's heated stare. And by heated, I mean furious, not hell bent on seduction. The image seared in my mind at that brief thought leaves me breathless.

"Arthur, a word." Rob leaves the room with Arthur following in his wake.

I can't very well chase after them to eavesdrop a second time without getting caught. My head weighs a ton and even with the medication, the pain stabs through my skull. I touch the cut once more and groan. What I want is a shower, some warm pajamas, and to curl up and sleep. Hopefully I'll wake up and I won't be trapped in 1985 with a grumpy businessman and his doctor friend as my only allies.

Reality weighs down on me. Do I want to return to the present? I mean after the bang-up year I had, I'd much rather be stranded in the middle ages than 2020. But it was more. I lost so much this past year, I considered ending it all.

Now I'm stuck in the past. Right where my beginning started, and I can't help but wonder if this is fate playing some cruel joke on me.

I slowly rise to my feet and walk to the floor length window and lose myself in the rising darkness beyond. As the last remnants of sunlight fade beyond the horizon, I press my face to the cold glass.

How the hell am I going to make this work? There must be some laws of physics and time I must be violating by being here. I can't imagine trying to live in a transported time wondering if I'm meddling with the fabric of the universe.

Take it one day at a time, I hear my mother whisper through my memories. One thing is certain, I will see my parents again, and that alone is worth the risk of a paradox and the wrath of the man in the other room who is now my only ally in this world.

With no money, no job, no apartment, I am at his mercy. A shiver of excitement grips me.

Be careful, my mind cautions. I catch a glimpse of my reflection in the glass and behind me, through the door, I see Arthur appear.

"I see you're going to be a handful." His disappointment echoes clearly in his heady baritone voice.

When I spin around, I sway at the quick motion and lean against the glass.

In a flash, he's by my side, his hands firmly planted around my waist. "Lie down before you fall down."

His words are harsh, but his gentle touch says something completely different, leaving an ache deep in my chest when he helps me onto the bed and backs away. "Stay there. I need to make a phone call."

I expect him to pull out a cell phone, but instead, he leaves the room. I squeeze my eyes closed. *Cell phones aren't a thing yet, idiot.*

Yeah, being stuck in 1985 is going to be more difficult than I thought if I expected to be able to maintain any semblance of normalcy.

CHAPTER FOUR

ARTHUR

It takes every ounce of effort not to shove Rob out the door and slam it in his face. Instead, I stewed while he lectured and guilted me into taking responsibility for this lost little lamb. Hah. Lamb, my ass. After he left, I found her staring out over the city when she should have been in bed resting. If I hadn't seen her unconscious firsthand, I would have thought it all an act. The question is, why go to all that trouble? What is her angle?

Rob may be blind to her wiles, but one look at those wide, mesmerizing eyes and I knew. This woman is trouble. Maybe it's my own bias. I don't exactly have a great track record with women, but none have given me a reason to trust them. Vultures and vixens, all of them. Well, except one. And unfortunately, she is the only one I can call for help right now.

I rake my hand across my face in irritation and retreat into the living room. Once I make this call, I'll never hear the end of it. But I don't have any other course of action. I lift the phone receiver to my shoulder and dial a number as familiar as my own. After a few lengthy rings, the line connects.

"Hello, this is Marcy Maxwell."

"Hi, Marcy."

"Arthur." Her business tone shifts to one of amusement. "Happy New Year."

I grunt and ignore the stabbing irritation in my skull. "You busy?"

"Just reorganizing my closets with Donna and Liana." She snaps the gum she's chewing. "Why?"

Taking a deep breath, I push forward. "I need a favor."

"Holy shit. Did hell freeze over? Who are you and what have you done with my brother?"

"Laugh it up." I growl knowing I'll never live this down.

She sobers quickly. "What can I do for you? Get you a new wardrobe? A blind date? Maybe find you a sense of humor?"

"I need you to make up a bag. Toiletries, makeup, and clothes." I brace myself for the deluge of questions I'm about to face and march into the gaping maw of hell. "For a woman."

"Get the hell out of here." She gasps. "Did you snag yourself a babe?"

"I'm not even going to dignify that with an answer." I sigh. "Can you do this for me?"

"Under two conditions." She snaps her gum again.

"Name them." I stare at my reflection in the window wondering if I haven't signed a contract with the devil.

"Nonna's blanket." She tuts when I groan. "And the recipe for her chicken noodle soup." Marcy knows exactly what she wants, which is why she's the most sought-after stylist in the city.

"Fine." I sit on the arm of the couch and carefully twist the cord so I don't knock the whole thing to the ground. "How fast can you be here?"

"As soon as you give me her measurements, I can be there in thirty."

My head spins. Measurements? What the hell? "I don't know her measurements, Marcy."

"Ask her, idiot." She tuts again in exasperation.

"Hold on." I set the phone down and head toward the bedroom. Inside, I find my uninvited guest staring at the ceiling chewing on her lip.

"Everything okay?" she asks when I open the door.

"Of course." I bristle. No, it goddamn isn't okay. You've upended my plans and you're lying in my bed. I bite my tongue and ignore the frustration curdling in the back of my throat. "What are your measurements?"

Her eyes widen and she sits up enough to meet my gaze fully. "Why do you need those?"

"You can't wear the same clothes for days on end and I doubt you'll fit in mine."

"I wear a large top and a size fourteen jeans." She brushes her hair away from her eyes.

"Shoes?" I add taking mental note and trying not to imagine those curves I now know she's hiding beneath her baggy sweater.

"Eights."

I nod and leave the room, closing the door behind me. Shit. This can't be good. It's bad enough I don't know anything about this woman and here she is tormenting me without even trying.

I snatch the phone off the table. "Large top, size fourteen jeans, and size eight shoe. That work?"

"I can make it work for now." She sounds almost disappointed in my clipped response. "I'll be over in thirty minutes. Ciao."

After I hang up the phone, I stare blankly at the new television and state of the art stereo system sitting like huge bricks stacked against the wall. I don't know why I bought them. I never watch television or listen to music. The architecture firm takes up all of my time. My gaze drifts to the bedroom. At least it did.

If I had known what was waiting for me on the other side of the door at the office this morning, I wouldn't have gone in. A fleeting memory of Kate's soft body pressed against me makes me pause. I remember the sweet, teasing scent of a tropical island drifting up from her hair and pulling me closer. Guilt crashes over me again when I remember the sight of her crumpled on the floor, blood marring her pale forehead.

I shoot to my feet and pace the floor. Rob, being astute and noble as ever, has a valid point. I was responsible for her injury, therefore I am responsible for her recovery. Until we get some answers as to where she came from and who she is, I guess I'll have to cope with the inconvenience.

This time I knock on the bedroom door.

"Come in." Her voice filters through the wood.

When I push open the door, I expect to find her exactly where I left her moments before. Instead, she's sitting on the edge of the bed staring out the window. I clear my throat and stalk to the far wall where the en suite bathroom is located. I flip on the light and turn to face her.

"Here's the bathroom." I stuff my hands into my pockets

and lean against the door.

She's still staring out the window as if entranced by the city lights flickering outside. "Thank you."

Silence fills the void between us. "I'll be in the other room if you require anything else." Without waiting for a response, I leave the bedroom, making sure to close the door behind me.

I unfasten the buttons on my wrists and roll my sleeves up. In the kitchen, I gather some vegetables from the refrigerator. Breakfast was a cup of coffee and a bagel from the shop on the corner. In all the chaos, I completely forgot about lunch. A reminder my stomach punctuates with a loud grumble.

Chopping peppers and onions gives me something to do with my hands. I'm careful not to let my mind wander too deeply into the mess I find myself mired. I pop a slice of pepper in my mouth as I set a pan on the stovetop. My recipe isn't quite as good as Nonna's, but it works when I don't have the time for a full ragu simmer. As I fill the pot with water for the pasta, the door buzzes. Quickly, I toss the onions in the first pot and let the hot oil work it's magic.

When I open the door, I'm stunned to find not only my sister, but her two associates carrying bags in her wake.

"Arthur." Marcy regards me with a smile and a once over. "You look like a train wreck."

"Hello, Marcy." I nod to her associates. "Liana. Donna. Come in," They pass without hesitation when I step aside.

"Smells good." My sister sniffs the air. "Nonna's ragu?"

"No one has that kind of free time." I disappear into the kitchen and stir the onions ensuring they caramelize evenly.

Marcy leans against the counter next to the stove. "So, dish. Who's the chick?"

"Your slang has gotten worse." I scowl. "Working with all those rock stars and celebrities is starting to rot your brain."

"You're a grumpy old man. Don't take your issues out on me." She sneaks a pepper from the cutting board and snaps it between her teeth. "So, where is she?"

"In the bedroom." I regret the words the moment they leave my mouth.

Marcy's brows shoot straight up. "You sly dog. That was fast!"

"It's not what you think." I groan and backpedal knowing she won't let this rest now or ever if I don't tell her the truth. In the fewest possible words, I explain what happened at the office and how I brought the woman here. I assure her Rob came and offered his professional advice.

"Are you kidding me? Professional advice, my ass." She rolls her eyes and snorts.

"You and Rob have your little rivalry or whatever it is, but he's my friend and a doctor. As much as his advice wasn't what I wanted to hear..." I shrug and let the implication slide into oblivion.

"You feel guilty for whacking her over the head and knocking her out." Marcy chuckles. "Good. You should." She snatches another pepper as I pour wine into the onions to deglaze them.

I glare my sister wishing I had another female in my life who I could have called, but unfortunately, this is the curse of being a man married to his work. "I don't need you to heap more guilt onto my shoulders as well, Marcy." I jab my wooden spoon in her direction. "Just take the clothes and stuff into the bedroom."

"I bet you didn't even tell her I was coming or who I am." She winks and disappears before I can stop her.

Shit. I didn't tell her. I hang my head and chase after my sister. "Liana, keep an eye on the sauce, would you?" I motion to my sister's assistant who gives me a strange look.

Marcy spins around at my command and glowers. "Don't tell her what to do. She works for me, not you."

"Shit." I step between my sister and the bedroom door. "No, okay, you win. I didn't tell her you were coming or who you were. Just...give me a minute."

I open the door and find the room empty. The sound of running water echoes behind the closed bathroom door. My eyes drift closed. If she's lying on the shower floor unconscious, I'll never forgive myself.

"Go stir your ragu, genius. I got this." Marcy steps toward

the bathroom door and knocks.

Liana and Donna carry the bags into the bedroom as I head back to the kitchen. Well, the new year is off to a promising start. I've accosted, kidnapped, and possibly killed a stranger. Fantastic.

Even better, my best friend and my sister are witnesses to my failure. Fucking perfect. What else could possibly go wrong?

In the kitchen, my wine has evaporated leaving burned onions sticking to the bottom of the pot. I rinse it out and start over. Maybe I should order food from Lorenzo's and drown my misery in a bottle of chianti.

The scream from the bedroom makes my heart stop.

CHAPTER FIVE
KATHERINE

The shower in this place can fit three people, at least. I lean against the tan tiles and let the water run through my hair, sluicing over the sore lump my generous host gave me earlier. It wasn't his fault, honestly, if it happened the way he says it did. Damn it. I wanted to ask him about it when he came back, but the scowl on his face drove all thoughts of conversation from my mind.

While my head ached, the pain seems to have dimmed enough to tolerate being on my feet. I pray I don't pass out while I'm in the shower. The thought of not showering crossed my mind, but one look in the mirror confirmed the truth. I'm a hot mess. Dried blood caked against my scalp, blotchy skin, and dark circles highlight my eyes. Before I could stop myself, I was naked and in the shower.

I use some of the soap and lather a washcloth. The subtle hint of lemon zest reminds me of the soap Nanna used to have at her house. My hair will be a beast to untangle without the proper shampoo and conditioner. I use whatever's in the shower knowing I'll smell like him. But the thought isn't a complete turn off.

The thought of my unwilling host even smiling is almost comical. He looked every inch the disapproving dad. Hah. Dad. Daddy. He certainly is daddy as fuck which seems super creepy considering the fact I haven't even been born yet.

I chuckle and slip on the tile. My heart lurches and I brace myself against the glass door until my body is in complete control once more. Shit. I need to pay attention or I'll die naked in a stranger's shower. What a thought.

Carefully, I finish rinsing my hair and toss it over my

shoulder.

"Don't use his shampoo. Damn. We'll never get those curls sorted."

I spin around and slip again, this time falling on my bare ass. There's a hazy figure of a woman on the other side of the glass.

"Christ, I didn't mean to scare you. I knew that bastard didn't tell you." She mutters the last sentence under her breath, but I can hear her clearly.

I cross my arms over my naked breasts and cross my legs for all the good it does at hiding my childbearing hips.

"Oh honey, don't be modest. I've seen more naked women than Hugh Heffner." She slides open the door and I catch a glimpse of crimped hair and a neon headband as she sets some bottles on the rack inside the shower. "Try these. There's a leave in conditioner that's amazing." The door slides shut, but she doesn't leave.

"Uh..." I slowly climb to my feet and read the bottles provided. "Who are you?"

"Oh, sorry, sugar. I'm Marcy." She snaps her gum.

"Why are you here?" The moment the shampoo touches my hair it thanks me by allowing my fingers to comb through the stubborn curls.

"Cause I'm the best." She giggles to herself. "And I'm the only one Arthur calls when he's in freak out mode." She huffs. "Well, the only woman."

I rinse the soap out of my hair and listen with confusion. "I don't understand."

Marcy sighs. "I'll let you finish up. We'll talk once you're out of the shower." She moves toward the door. "Don't take too long."

While I'm thankful for the salon quality supplies, I still don't know who she is or why the hell Arthur called her. I finish my shower and wrap my head with a towel before bundling up with a second one. My head aches with the weight of the fabric and my ass hurts. I'll definitely have a bruise there tomorrow. Damn. My ego and my ass. Awesome.

In the bedroom, I stop at the sight of three women, two

lounging on the edge of the bed chatting and the third drawing the blinds across the windows. They all turn toward me.

"Awesome," Marcy says, rising to her feet. She's tall and willowy with dark hair and sparkling eyes. Her polka dot neon green shirt drapes over her shoulders and nips at her waist beneath a wide black belt.

It's like a bad dream where I'm trapped naked in an eighties music video with a bunch of strangers. I pull the towel tighter around my chest.

"Donna. Grab the kit. We'll give her some beauty essentials." Marcy snaps her fingers like she forgot something. Finally, she grins. "Liana, let's try a few of the pieces you picked. Not feeling the glam vibe, but I think she's got the bod for the rock look."

"What are you doing?" I protest when Marcy hooks her arm through mine, dislodging my towel.

"Don't worry about it. We're professionals." This time I see the lime green shadow and flecks of gold glitter at the corners of her eyes.

"Professional what?"

"Fashion mavens." She cocks her head and inspects me, walking around me twice before nodding. "Trust me."

"You still haven't told me who you are." I squeal when she pulls the towels off my head. A mass of heavy wet curls falls across my face hiding my shameful blush.

"Marcy. I told you." Two pieces of silk and lace are pressed into my hands. "Try these."

I tug on the lace demi bra and high wasted panties. Lord, these are a blast from the past.

Someone nudges my side. "Sit down, hon. Let me take care of those curls for you." Donna, I think she said her name was, pushes me toward the chair where she begins detangling my curls. I point out the tender spot on my scalp which she carefully avoids.

"Arthur didn't specify how long you'll be staying or what you'll need, so I brought a variety. They should fit, but if they don't, call me and I'll change them out. They're all last season's wardrobe." Marcy flips through the pile of clothing growing on the bed.

The colors and styles are most definitely last century's wardrobe, that's for sure. I bite my tongue as she shows me each outfit combination. Oh, my God. I remember dress up for the eighties day at school, but I don't remember these patterns and fabrics. What is wrong with this decade?

An hour later, I'm exhausted. She's wrapped me in some kind of pink leggings and a billowy silk shirt. I wiggle, unfamiliar but not uncomfortable, with the new duds. Her word, not mine. I scramble through my mind for any memories of movies from the eighties in which I can pull references and slang. All I can think of is *Back to the Future* and *Top Gun*. Not helpful.

"Well, I think we've done our best, ladies." Marcy gestures to the other two women who wave as they step out of the room. "I'll let you get some rest." She smiles and this time it feels more genuine.

"Thank you." I glance at myself in the mirror one last time.

"Of course. It's the least I can do." She rests her hand on my shoulder. "If my brother gives you any crap, just give it right back to him."

My gaze meets hers in the reflection. "Arthur is your brother?"

"Well, yeah, duh." She laughs. "You didn't think we were together, did you?"

I study the carpet and a wave of shame washes over me. "Yeah. I did. Sorry."

"No reason to be sorry. I thought he told you." She snaps her gum again. "Guess he owes me double." Her hug startles me for a moment, but it feels like heaven and I sink into it. "Just give me a ring if you need me to kick his ass."

"I will." A sense of loss envelops me as she steps back.

"Come on, let's show him how I work my magic." Marcy pulls me into the living room by the hand. "Hey, Arthur."

On cue, Arthur steps out of the far room. My heart stops at the sight of him. His shirtsleeves are pushed up exposing strong forearms. The vee of skin at his throat draws my attention upward to his angled jaw and full lips. Oh God, he's hotter. How is that possible?

His sharp gaze narrows as it skims over my body. "It works."

I want to grab the vase off the mantel and hurl it at him. Really, so much work for this pathetic reaction. I mean, honestly, it wasn't to impress him in the first place, but my ego is already battered.

"You're welcome." She gives my hand a squeeze. "Get some rest. Ciao!"

Without further fanfare, the three women leave the penthouse surrendering me to the company of the sexy, grumpy Daddy. I shake my head. No. Not going there. Never going there.

"Are you hungry?" he asks, stuffing his hands into his pockets.

The question pulls me from my twisted thoughts. "Yes. I'm starving."

His lips twitch, but he remains stoic. "Come into the kitchen."

The penthouse has a spacious openness making it feel grand and leaving little privacy when in the main common areas. The living room and kitchen sit side by side, although the kitchen is elevated a fraction making it the main functionality of the room. There's a small dining area off to the right along with several closed doors. The opposite side is where his bedroom sits along with a glass door leading to what looks like a balcony with greenery. How did I miss that? Curiosity pulls at me, but the tantalizing scents emanating from the kitchen draw me back to the moment and my hunger.

He hands me a plate and piles pasta mixed with sauce on it. "There's cheese here." He gestures to the counter beside the stove.

I slide past him, my hip grazing his thigh. The touch is innocent enough, but a weighted undercurrent pulls me toward him. I force myself away. After sprinkling on a healthy dose of parmesan, I cross through the kitchen to the dining room and sit near the window to get the best view while I eat.

Once Arthur joins me, I dig in. The sauce coats the noodles perfectly. My headache eases with each bite. I must have been hungrier than I realized.

Arthur's staring at me. I can't tell if he's more horrified by my manners or my appetite. He arches a brow.

"Sorry. It's just..." I lick my lips and smile. "It's really good."

He takes a bite.

I focus on eating slower. "Did you make this?"

He nods. "My Nonna's recipe."

"Nonna?" I ask wiping a stray bit of sauce from my cheek.

"Italian for grandma. She emigrated when she was young."

"Wow." I stuff more pasta in my mouth so I don't trip over my words and say something that makes the universe implode. Silence descends like a heavy fog.

I finish my last bite and push the plate away. Satisfied and grateful. But the silence is killing me. The man across the table doesn't seem interested in talking any more than I do, but I am curious. Maybe my curiosity is what contributed the events which led me to the top of the Empire State Building in the first place. It doesn't matter. I don't have any friends here and we're stuck together, so I might as well make the best of it.

"So, Arthur, what do you do?"

"I'm an architect." He swirls the wine in his glass, and I stare at my own water with regret.

Then it clicks. "Wait, you work at Lincoln Architecture Firm?"

"I started it." Arthur sips his wine taking full measure of me as he does so.

My face heats and I remember the paper I found lying on the ground outside the office. "Arthur Maxwell," I mutter under my breath and hide my face in my hands. "Of course."

"Your amnesia must be clearing up. I never told you my surname." His eyes glint with challenge.

"When I was outside your office, I found a paper on the ground. I bent down to pick it up and saw that name...your name on it. Right before you knocked me out with the door and kidnapped me." I fold my arms across my chest and hold his gaze.

"It was an accident." He leans forward and braces his bare forearms on the table. The light catches the hint of gray starting at his temples and my body goes into hyper alert.

Shit, am I supposed to be scared or horny right now? I'm confused. I shove both away with force and clear my throat. "Accident or not. It happened. Nothing we can do about it now."

"I find it difficult to believe you can remember your name and the fact you have no family or friends to call, but nothing else."

I swallow convulsively. "Well, I don't, and that's all I know." It's not a lie per se, but it's definitely not the truth. I pray he doesn't press me further.

Arthur looks more skeptical than before.

"I'll be out of your hair in a few days. I'll find a job and pay you back for the inconvenience," I lie. How the hell am I going to legally work? I don't exist. "If you want, I can cook, I'll clean, whatever I need to do. I don't want to be an inconvenience."

He harumphs. "Too late."

It stings, but I brush it off and take the opening I've recognized as the perfect opportunity. "Do you need help at the office? I can answer phones or run errands."

He scoffs and takes another drink. "No. The last thing I need is you at the office as well as my apartment."

I stand and collect the dishes. "Fine. I offered."

Without waiting for a reply, I carry the dirty plates to the sink to clean them. I can tell when my company isn't appreciated. The familiar feeling bites even more now because I'm completely out of my element.

As I wash, Arthur sets his glass next to the sink. His presence and the spicy cologne I'm beginning to associate with him distract me. He turns and leans against the counter, crossing his arms over his broad chest.

"Today has been strange for both of us." He exhales sharply. "Stay. Recover. We'll figure something out."

"I can't stay here and do nothing. There must be some way I can pay you." I meet his gaze and realize my mistake instantly. He's close. Too close. My heart races faster.

"Your eyes." He blinks twice before finishing his thought. "They're two different colors."

"Yeah," I murmur. Heterochromia runs in the family, but I can't tell him because I'm supposed to have amnesia. Shit.

His lips curl into a smile and my fucking heart stops beating. No man should look so delicious when he smiles. Arthur's smile could tempt a woman to sin and then lure her to the end of the universe. As quickly as it appeared, it vanishes.

Oh, sweet baby Yoda. I can't fantasize about my dad's boss. I refuse to flirt with him, no matter how sexy and brooding he is. What the hell am I going to do?

CHAPTER SIX

ARTHUR

What the hell has gotten into me? I take a step back and shake this unnerving attraction away before it can dig its talons into me.

This woman. Damn it. I'm no closer to knowing who she really is or where she came from, but I can't deny the tension building between us. Watching her savor the dinner I made from scratch has me pinned between pride and lust. I can't reveal how much she affects me. Mostly because I don't understand how that's even possible.

How the hell did I get to this point? As she washes the dishes, I war with the conflict tearing apart my conscience. I don't need this complication, not now, not ever. The women in my life, my mother, grandmother, hell, even my sister, would never let me live a day longer if they discovered I turned this vulnerable woman out into the street without money or protection.

The vixen doesn't even need protection. The fire in her eyes when I challenged her at dinner revealed a passion hidden deep within. She would put up a fight, and the thought intensifies this desire I never expected.

I shift my weight trying to hide the effect she has on my libido. I may be an asshole, but I'm not blind. She's fucking gorgeous. My sister definitely knows her craft. She took what was already present and highlighted it with ease. The billowy silk shirt amplifies those curves I knew lay beneath her oversized sweater. I felt every one of them pressed against me earlier when I carried her.

"I'm going to take a shower," I mutter before pushing past her. I'm halfway across the room when I hear her call out.

"Thank you for dinner."

My heart softens a fraction, but I just wave in acknowledgement and keep walking. Once I'm safely locked in the bathroom, I lean against the door and take a few deep breaths. The sweet, floral scent of the soap she used lingers in the room. I pinch my eyes closed.

She's marking everything, leaving reminders of herself across my apartment. After years of living alone, blissfully untethered by marriage or even a steady relationship, having someone living in such close quarters is more challenging than I remember. It's only temporary. By mid-month, she'll be out of my life permanently. Why does the thought of her leaving piss me off?

I tear open my shirt with more force than necessary and glare at my own reflection. A long, cold shower should help me refocus. I have a firm to run and projects to finish. This year I intend to land the contract which will set both my firm and myself up indefinitely. Early retirement is sounding pretty good. Maybe a new venture will come along and carry me into my golden years.

It sounds ridiculous. I'm barely forty. I have my whole life ahead of me.

The cool spray of the shower rinses away thoughts of Kate and the events of the day. After a long soak, I step from the shower and dry off, wrapping the towel around my hips. I crack the door open expecting to find Kate, but the room is empty.

I pull a pair of sleep pants from the dresser and slip them on. Normally, that's all I wear, but I don a sweatshirt. The fabric rasps against my skin, but I shrug off the annoyance.

In the living room, Kate is bundled beneath a blanket on the couch where she's made a bed of sorts from blankets I had in the closet. *Make yourself at home why don't you.* I bite back the words when I notice her eyes are closed.

The thought of her rifling through my apartment should have irritated me more than it did. I cock my head and study her. The crochet afghan lay against her chin. All I can see is her face surrounded by a halo of dark curls. Innocent? Most assuredly not. This woman has burrowed beneath my skin, and the knowledge doesn't sit well with me.

"Take the bed." I tug on the blanket around her feet. "I'll sleep out here."

Her eyes fly open and fix on me with open suspicion. "No. I'm fine here."

"After my actions today, it's the least I can do. Take the bed. You need to recover."

"I can recover on the couch as well as the bed." She clutches the blanket tighter.

I grab a handful of the blanket and pull it off her.

"No!" She squeals when it slips from her hands and reveals her whole body. Her hands immediately grapple to cover her bare skin. The silk and lace camisole and shorts leave nothing to the imagination.

Sweet merciful God, what is she wearing? And why the hell would my sister give her sexy lingerie to sleep in rather than functional pajamas? I resist the urge to call my sister and instead toss the blanket back over Kate's shivering form.

"What the hell is Marcy thinking?" I shake my head. "You'll freeze in that getup."

Without waiting for her response, I stalk back into my bedroom and pull out the smallest set of pajamas I have. I typically buy sets but only end up wearing the bottoms. They're an unflattering plaid with red and blue stripes, but they're warmer than what she's wearing.

I return to the living room and toss the clothes on her lap. Her eyes widen when she unfolds the fabric. The motion draws attention to the silken camisole as it slips over her shoulder revealing the tempting curve of her breast.

"I don't need you freezing to death. Rob will kill me."

"Thanks." She stands up and the blanket falls away for a brief second as she struggles to wrap it around herself. The silk clings to the plush curves of her body.

With the effort of a saint, I turn and retreat into the kitchen to get a glass of water.

The sound of my bedroom door closing fills me with relief.

I lean against the cabinet and set my water aside. My cock twitches as my mind replays the moment the blanket drops. I groan and adjust myself regretting I didn't take the opportunity to relieve this sexual need when I was in the shower. As if it would have helped, I scoff.

After I finish the water, I flop down onto the couch where she made her little bed. The fabric is still warm and the tantalizing scent of her soap teases my nose. I close my eyes and visions of silk and lace sliding from Kate's body fill my mind. I grit my teeth. Great, now I'm painfully hard.

"You tricked me."

I open my eyes and Kate's standing over me, her hands on her hips, my pajamas hanging from her luscious curves, her full lips upturned in a scowl.

"I didn't trick you." I shift a pillow across my lap to hide my uncomfortable situation. "Those pajamas are much more comfortable, aren't they?"

Kate nods. "Yes, but I can't take your bed."

"You will." I fix her with my most intimidating and unwavering stare. "Go. I'll sleep here."

She huffs, her cheeks flaring with color, and her eyes flashing with challenge. "Fine. I'll sleep on the floor."

When she moves to kneel, I launch to my feet and snatch her by the arm. "Why must you be so stubborn?"

She glares up at me and tries to wrench herself from my grip. "You're the one who's being stubborn!"

Damn it. I snatch her by the waist and lift her over my shoulder.

"Put me down!" She squirms and writhes trying to free herself. My arm bands her legs down to keep her from kicking.

After two steps she's shouting profanities that would make a sailor blush. Without thinking, I bring my palm down hard on her ass. The satisfying crack echoes through the room. She stills completely.

"Now, settle down before I drop you." I stalk the rest of the way into the bedroom and toss her onto the bed.

Her indignant grunt ignites a surge of pride. She's a fighter, and I'm enjoying it much more than I should be.

"That's not how you treat someone with a head injury." She crawls to a sitting position on the bed and glares.

"You'll live." I jab my finger toward the bed. "Now, go to sleep."

Her gaze drifts over me pausing halfway down my body. She gasps and her gorgeous eyes widen as they meet mine.

Shit. There's no hiding it now. I prop my hands on my hips. "Is there a problem?"

She shakes her head so hard her curls obscure the blush creeping into her cheeks.

"I didn't think so."

As much as I want to join her in the bed and take full advantage of my situation, I turn and leave the room, slamming the door behind me.

I turn off the lights and settle on the couch, pulling the warmest blanket over me. Taking a few deep breaths, I attempt to cool the heat raging through me. My body reacts of its own will, and I smooth my hand over my cock. The movement only aggravates the need pummeling my system.

No. I refuse to succumb to this base sexual need. I don't know her. She doesn't know me. We are not friends. We're certainly not lovers. And hopefully in a week, we'll never cross paths again.

But as I lay in the dark staring at the ceiling, I hear my conscience whisper through the stillness. *Is this what you really want? Or do you want to see where the other path leads?*

Irritated, I roll onto my side. The other path can only lead to trouble. Curvy, soft, intoxicating trouble. Only a mad man would follow it.

CHAPTER SEVEN
KATHERINE

After a horrible night unable to sleep thanks to the unnecessary sexual attraction blossoming between Arthur and me, I must have hit a wall, or a door with my luck, because the next thing I know it's nine a.m. The makeshift bed on the couch lay empty and a note sits next to the still warm pot of coffee in the machine.

At work. My number is 555-8940. Use only in an emergency. Do not leave the apartment. Make yourself at home.

I toss the paper aside. Damn it. I had every intention of badgering him into letting me come with him to the office. I want to see my dad.

The note stares up at me. I read it again. It's no declaration of undying love, but deep beneath the brusque sentences, there's a glimpse of concern for my wellbeing. Maybe he's trying. I don't know.

Last night confused the hell out of me. One minute I can almost feel the sparks flying between us and the next he's built a brick wall ten feet high. The expression on his face when he saw the pajamas his sister brought. Oh, holy night. He looked ready to jump me then and there. But a cool displeasure smothered whatever heat ignited in that brief moment.

The way he tossed me over his shoulder and threw me on the bed. Hot. The way he dismissed me and left me completely confused. Well, dick move on his part.

I grab a cup of coffee and something to nibble before planting my butt in front of the TV. After messing with the ancient entertainment system, I finally get the damn thing turned on. I need something to distract me from the fact I'm attracted to my father's boss.

Three hours of non-stop soap operas is enough to rot anyone's brain. I rotate through the channels three times until I realize there's nothing good on television during the day. Not only was this true in my time but also in the past it seems.

I groan at the manufactured drama on the television. I don't even know which one this is. *Days of our Lives. Young and the Restless.* Hell, it could be *Dallas* for all I know. It's so over the top. I groan. How the hell did Nanna watch this garbage?

I click through it again and find MTV. Like actual MTV playing music videos. I instantly recognize the song. REO Speedwagon playing "Can't Fight This Feeling." I stare at the television entranced by the video. I've heard the song a million times, but I don't think I've ever seen the video. The lyrics return without hesitation. Oh man, the power of an eighties rock ballad.

I crank up the volume and sing along as I wander into the kitchen to find a snack. Inside the cabinet I find a bag of Doritos and a box of Famous Amos chocolate chip cookies. Score! There's only juice and water in the refrigerator. The cup of coffee and toast I ate this morning has long since worn off.

After tucking my snacks under one arm, I carry the juice and a glass into the living room. The bed I made the night before is still there. Blanket thrown over the back of the couch haphazardly. I pick it up and wrap it around me before settling down onto the couch.

The spicy scent of Arthur creates a cocoon around me. I nestle deeper into the fabric. Why does he have to smell so damn good?

Ten minutes of music videos and I'm nodding off. Just as I snuggle against the pillow and give in to the exhaustion, the phone rings.

I bolt upright and search the room. Where the hell is the phone?

It rings again and I see it sitting on a glass table beside the couch.

"Hello?" I nearly knock the whole contraption to the ground. Damn corded phones! Don't they have cordless yet? He's rich enough.

"I must have the wrong number. I was looking for Arthur," a woman's voice purrs through the receiver.

"No, this is the right number." I cradle the phone in both hands. "He's at work right now. Can I take a message?"

Silence fills the line.

"Hello? Are you still there?"

"I see Arthur hasn't wasted any time finding some hussy to warm his bed," the woman hisses.

Stunned, I choke on my reply before getting it out. "Excuse me?"

"You heard me, tramp. Moving in on another woman's territory, huh?"

I blink twice completely blanking on how to reply. "You misunderstand..."

"No. You misunderstand. Arthur is mine. So, you'd best get your shit and get out," she growls into the other line.

"Lady, I don't know who you are or what the hell you're smoking, but you have issues." I slam the phone down so hard it makes me flinch. Damn, that was satisfying. Ending a call on an iPhone doesn't have quite the same effect.

The soap opera drama has somehow transferred from the television and into my life. Great. I flop down onto the couch and burrow beneath the blanket once more.

With the music playing in the background, I find myself drifting off. Exhaustion plus the warmth of the blanket and his scent lull me into a contented state. I fall into dreamland and find my dad waiting for me.

He's wearing a dark pinstripe suit with a crimson tie standing in the oversized window overlooking the city. A blinding smile transforms his dour expression when he sees me. I run toward him with my arms open. He scoops me up and spins me around.

I'm a little girl again. Clinging to him, I'm lost in the moment. He sets me down and holds my gaze. His eyes brim with love and pride. One blue while the other is nearly engulfed in amber. The eyes I see reflected in the mirror every day.

"I love you, Dad." My voice cracks. "I miss you."

"Me too, Peanut." His joyful smile takes on a sad hue before he steps away. "Don't cry. We'll see each other again soon." His outline fades against the sunset over the city until all I see is the imposing presence of the Empire State Building.

"Kate," a familiar, imposing voice rumbles behind me.

I spin around and see Arthur leaning against the wall. The sunset plays across his features casting half of his face into shadow. He's wearing the same suit as Dad, but it fits him differently. Broader, more powerful. Intimidating. Sexy as hell. He uncrosses his arms and stalks toward me.

My back hits the glass. He pins me against it. His scent, his heat, his presence...they disorient me. My heart races, and I fear it will tear free from my chest.

Arthur's gaze drifts over me, a slow wandering perusal, before locking with mine. A crooked smile pulls at his lips. "You're mine now, Katherine." His hands grip my shoulders as he leans closer, his mouth a breath from mine.

"Kate."

Somewhere in the haze I hear my name. Before I feel the press of Arthur's kiss, I'm tumbling through the darkness.

"Kate."

I wrench my eyes open to find Arthur staring down at me. His hands grip my shoulders. He sighs with relief.

"Thank God." He releases me and rakes his hand through his hair. "I wasn't sure you were going to wake up." He stands and pulls his tie loose. "Must have been some dream."

Consciousness slaps me in the face like a cold winter gust of wind. I sit up and shake my head.

"What do you mean?" I clear my throat.

Arthur tugs the tie from his suit and unbuttons the top of his shirt baring a hint of skin at his throat. "You didn't want to wake up. Must have been a good dream."

My face heats. "Yeah." I turn my gaze away, unable to quell the thirst building at the sight of him practically doing a striptease compounded with the haunting memory of the dream kiss. Damn it.

"I'm gonna change." He walks toward the bedroom, giving

me a full view of his ass clad in fitted dress pants.

Sweet mother of Captain America, that ass.

"Would you please set the table? I brought dinner. Hope you like Chinese food." He gestures toward the kitchen with one hand before disappearing into the bedroom.

I press my hands to my face. Yup. Flaming hot. I'm sure it's a hideous shade of maroon. Great. Fanfuckingtastic. Is it possible to die from embarrassment? I don't know if I can even have a conversation with him now. Not after a sinful, sexy dream starring him. These thoughts need to stop. He's too old for me.

But is he really? The question pops unbidden to my mind flashing in big bold neon font. I need to be honest with myself. I'm stuck in 1985 indefinitely. Unless whatever powers that brought me here suddenly decide my time is up and they beam me right back to 2020.

I shake my head. No. There's nothing there for me. Not now.

I sound insane. Why would I be better off in the past?

A million reasons, the voice in my head whispers. I shush it with a wave of my hand and climb from the comfy nest on the couch. Darkness has already fallen over the city. I blink a few times and glance at the clock. Six p.m. Holy shit! I slept the day away.

In the kitchen I gather plates and silverware. On the dining room table there's an assortment of containers. I glance at the names on the top as I set the dishes on the table.

"I wasn't sure what you liked. So, I got a few of the basics," Arthur says from behind me.

Steeling myself, I turn and smile. "It looks great. Thanks."

"I was going to call, but one of my meetings ran late." He grabs a bottle of wine from the refrigerator and two glasses. "You want some?"

"Yes, please." I sit down and open the containers. "Unless you think I shouldn't. Rob did say I shouldn't drink."

"It's been twenty-four hours. I think you're good." He grins. "One glass won't kill you."

A grin. Be still my damn heart. Who knew one simple action

could make someone twenty times more attractive? I don't know if I can resist him if he keeps revealing these little hidden treasures. I nod because I can't trust the words to not come out of my mouth sounding like *please take me to bed and ravish me now*.

As I put food on our plates and he pours the wine, a silent awkwardness falls between us.

"*Buon appetito*." He gestures, raising his glass.

I tap mine to his and sip the refreshing white wine. It has a delightful fruity taste, but I'm sure it's not nearly as heady as Arthur's mouth. I'm riveted by it as he sips his wine.

"Something wrong?" he asks, setting the glass aside.

"No." I take a bite of lo mien and chew thoughtfully trying to desperately avoid fantasizing about my dad's boss. "Oh, you got a phone call today."

"Is that so?" He takes a bite of chicken.

"Yes. A woman called."

Arthur set his fork aside. "Shit." He leans his elbows on the table and exhales sharply. "I hope she wasn't rude."

"Well, she called me a hussy and a tramp. But I've been called worse." I shrug.

"I'm sorry."

"It's not your fault." I take another bite. "Your girlfriend?"

He scoffs. "Not really. We dated a few times. Social functions around town. But nothing serious."

I laugh. "Well, she never got the memo."

"What do you mean?"

"That woman thinks whatever you two have is the real deal." I break it to him as honestly as I can. "I guarantee she was expecting you to put a ring on it."

Arthur shakes his head and laughs. "A ring on what?"

I wag my left hand and point to my ring finger. "On this."

His eyes narrow. "I guess I'll have to clarify our agreement then it seems."

"Is everything a business arrangement with you?" I ask, genuinely curious as to the innerworkings of his mind.

"Yes." He replies without hesitation and takes another bite of food.

The wheels in my mind spin. "Then how about we make an arrangement?"

Arthur nearly chokes on his fried rice. "What?"

"An arrangement. Between you and me."

Skepticism seems so natural on his expression. "What are you proposing?"

"I need a job and a place to stay."

He grins and leans forward. "What's in it for me?"

"I keep the bitch off your back." I shrug. "Plus, I'm a whiz at Microsoft Office."

"I'm not sure what the hell you're talking about." He leans back and studies me carefully. "But it seems I could use a bit of help at the office. My secretary quit this morning and the temp agency is shorthanded."

"No problem. I can handle it."

A wicked grin crosses Arthur's lips and I'm transported to the dream instantly. My heart pounds and my appetite for dinner is replaced by something much more carnal.

"Oh, I'm sure you can, Kate."

I walked into that one, and I don't regret it. But I'm about to see my dad again. This now overshadows the longings I'd much rather not inspect too carefully.

CHAPTER EIGHT
ARTHUR

Those springs are lethal. I don't know if I can spend one more night on the torture device also known as my sofa. It's barely six thirty, and I'm already up with a cup of coffee staring out the window. The blue haze of dawn breaking into a cacophony of orange and pinks lays over the horizon.

I debate leaving her at the apartment again, even though I agreed to her insane plan. Truth is, I'm not against having her in the office. I could use the help. The real concern is how the hell I'm going to function with her being a physical distraction in my space all day.

There is no logical reason for this attraction. I mean, of course, she's gorgeous as well as quick witted. I even enjoy the way she challenges me rather than accepting her fate meekly. But none of this explains the chemistry building between us. It's been forty-eight hours since we met, for Christ's sake.

The alarm rings in the bedroom. I pour a second cup of coffee and take it in hoping it will entice her to get up.

The bed's empty. I turn off the alarm and knock on the bathroom door.

"I'll be done in a minute," she calls out.

"Take your time," I shout back. "I brought you…" The door opens and my eyes drift over the woman standing before me. Kate's wearing a black pencil skirt and a flowy green blouse with a wide belt tucked around the narrowest part of her hourglass figure. Her dark curls are tamed in a bun and loose tendrils frame her face. I don't know what kind of witchcraft my sister utilized, but holy shit, the transformation is night and day.

"Coffee." She sighs with contentment and takes the mug from my hand. "Thanks." The look on her face as she sips the brew is pure bliss.

I'm half-jealous of a coffee mug the way her lips press against the porcelain. Would they taste sweet with a hint of the earthy caffeinated beverage? Ignoring the persistent fantasy, I clear my throat.

"We leave at seven thirty." Without waiting for her response, I push past her and shut the bathroom door creating a solid barrier between us.

Instead of allowing myself to think about Kate and this growing fascination, I run through the mental checklist for my day. I have two meetings with clients and one with the head of the development office. It will only be me today since Victor is out of the office for the remainder of the week. We can schedule a meeting for Monday morning to discuss plans for the month and assess the quarterly goals for the year.

Twenty minutes later, I'm showered, shaved, and dressed. As I fasten the watch around my wrist, my reflection in the mirror convinces me I'm prepared to face whatever the day may bring. When I open the door and find Kate sitting on the loveseat flipping through the paper, my confidence trips and falls face first into rush hour traffic.

"Do you have a coat that doesn't look like it came from a thrift bin?" I cross the room and open the closet near the front door.

"Yes, your sister gave me one." She stands and retrieves the oversized monstrosity I found her in.

"Why are you wearing this one then?" I frown. "It looks ancient." I pull it toward me and check the tag. "It's a man's." An unfamiliar pang of jealousy nags at the back of my mind.

"It's much warmer." She smiles and pulls the worn wool jacket around her shoulders. "Plus, it was my dad's."

"He's probably freezing."

A forlorn expression steals her smile and she drops her gaze. "Yeah." She shakes her head. "Anyway, shall we go? I don't want to be late on my first day."

The moment passes as quickly as it arrived. "I'm sure your new employer will understand."

I open the door, and she steps into the corridor, pausing to wait for me. Once we arrive at the ground floor, she grips my arm but quickly releases me.

"Sorry. I guess I'm more nervous than I thought."

"About what?" I hold the door for her and we step out into the street. The bustle of the city surrounds us and as usual it invigorates me, breathing life into my routine.

She doesn't respond. I turn to find her watching the people walking past the front of the building. Her wide eyes dart back and forth, her lips parted in awe.

"Something wrong?" I come alongside her and nudge her toward the car where Cyril is waiting.

"No." Kate shakes her head almost a bit too quickly but smiles when she sees my driver.

"I'm glad to see you've recovered, ma'am." Cyril tips his hat to her before shifting his attention to me. "Good morning, Mr. Maxwell."

"Kate, this is my driver Cyril."

"Nice to meet you." She shakes his hand.

Cyril reacts slowly, dumbfounded at her reaction. "Likewise." He grins. "If you need anything, don't hesitate to ask."

"When I asked you to swing by Grant and pick up my suit at the cleaners, you told me you're a driver, not a manservant." I shove my hands in my pockets and stare pointedly at my driver.

Cyril shrugs. "You're not a beautiful woman recovering from an injury, are you?"

Kate chuckles before climbing into the backseat of the car.

Pride and indignance rear their heads in unison at his snappy retort. "Careful, Cyril, or you'll be hard pressed to find another gig in the city once I fire you." I climb into the car behind her.

The driver scoffs. "Whatever you say, sir." The door closes, firmly punctuating his statement.

"I like him." Kate smiles.

I study her bright expression. This is the first time I've seen her smile. My heart stirs at the way her eyes crinkle at the corners and her grin reveals a small dimple in her right cheek.

"Well, don't. He's impertinent." I straighten my tie and face forward as the car turns into traffic.

Kate leans closer, her breath brushing against my ear. "You won't really fire him, will you?"

The teasing floral scent of her soap sinks into my brain, and the caress of her breath creates a riot of desperation shooting through me like fireworks over the bay. My fist clenches to keep from reaching for her.

I shrug a shoulder noncommittally, not trusting myself to face her or even respond.

She leans back against the seat and stares out the window. The ride to the office continues in silence. It takes me that long to reign my unruly thoughts into some semblance of cohesion.

Once we arrive at the office, the world around me clicks into synchronization. A calm settles over me, even with Kate, a factor of the unknown, by my side.

Gladys looks up from the typewriter when I open the door. Her smile faulters for a moment at the sight of Kate.

"Good morning, Mr. Maxwell." She abandons the typewriter and rises to her feet.

"Gladys, this is Kate. She'll be working as my temporary assistant for a few weeks until we find a permanent replacement." I keep the conversation simple and unfettered with details. "Would you please show her around and give her an idea of how we do things around here?"

"Of course, Mr. Maxwell," Gladys replies with a sincere smile. "Welcome, Kate."

"I'll be in my office preparing for my nine-thirty. Please hold all my calls." With a parting glance at Kate, I turn and barricade myself inside my office. I don't know what I was thinking bringing her to work with me. How the hell am I going to concentrate knowing she's running loose in my business where I found her snooping on New Year's Day?

I pinch the bridge of my nose. Doesn't matter. There's a reasonable explanation. When her memory returns, I'll ask her. Until then, there's nothing I can do except keep a close eye on her.

I hang up my jacket on the coat rack and pause. She mentioned her old, oversized coat belonged to her father. Is this a sign of her memory returning?

Bolstered by hope, I sit behind my desk and prepare for the upcoming meeting. As much as I want her to recover and move on, I can't ignore the pinch of regret at the thought of her leaving. Shaking my head, I focus on the papers before me and not on the woman who's fallen directly into my path and aroused these unnecessary desires.

CHAPTER NINE
KATHERINE

Being productive gives me life. Seriously. Ever since I lost my job in November, compounded by Mom's death shortly after, and then jackass breaking up with me right before Christmas, I've been adrift. Today, I feel like my life has purpose again, and that alone gives me hope.

I glance at Arthur's closed office door. He's been in and out of the conference room all day with various clients. While he's given direction and made requests, our interactions have been minimal. I can't say I'm not disappointed, because I am. I like having his sole attention.

Two stacks of papers sit twelve inches deep on my desk. My most pressing task today is to organize and file them. This I can handle. No problem.

Gladys smiles from across the room. She's sweet and friendly. Her humor reminds me of my mother. After Arthur left me in her capable hands, we became friends quickly. We're about the same age—a technicality, I know. She's worked at the firm since Arthur started it fifteen years ago, so she knows the ins and outs and what's expected of the staff.

Once I got the grand tour of the office, she explained the details of what my job entails and where to find supplies, files, and so forth. The office is so well organized, it makes my job easy. She directed me to take the desk outside Arthur's office and answer any incoming calls in between filing the paperwork piled on the desk.

The day passes quickly. More quickly than sitting in Arthur's apartment watching soap operas all day, that's for sure. In an era where Netflix and Google and the internet are distant dreams, having a job is certainly a welcoming diversion. I can't believe how different it feels not having those things at my fingertips. Even walking around without my phone makes me feel like I'm naked. I think I miss digital music most of all. Waiting for a familiar and loved song to play on the radio is painful. How did people survive monotony? The answer is obvious now. Work.

Gladys sashays across the room in her mauve dress with the wide padded shoulders and poufy blonde hair. Ugh, the fashion during this decade certainly leaves a lot to be desired.

"That's enough for today, hon." She smiles and grabs her purse and jacket from the closet. "How was your first day?"

"Good." I lean back and stretch. "Thank you for all your help."

"Any time. If you have any questions, don't hesitate to ask." She pulls the coat on and fluffs her hair over the collar.

"Aren't there three architects with the firm?" I ask, hedging around the one question I've been dying to ask all day. "I already know Mr. Maxwell and I met Mr. Brooks."

"Oh yeah, Mr. Cohen. He's out this week. Took his wife on a special trip." Her eyes glaze over at the thought. "Lucky woman. Mr. Cohen is a great guy. You'll like him."

"I'm sure I will." My heart constricts when she mentions Dad. I miss him so much I could burst. I'd been so hopeful at the thought of meeting him today.

"He'll be back in the office on Monday." She slips her purse over her shoulder. "You heading home now?"

"Not yet. Mr. Maxwell wanted me to stay until after he finishes this last meeting."

"Okay." She winks. "Don't let him take advantage of you. Maybe we can grab a drink after work one day next week."

"Sounds good to me. Thanks again, Gladys."

"Any time, honey." She waves before heading for the elevator.

I stand up and arch my back stretching to the right and then the left. I'll definitely need some yoga stretches added to my daily routine if I keep this up.

"You finished with the filing already?"

My heart stops at the sound of Arthur's voice behind me. I

whip around and find him leaning against the doorframe of his office with his brow arched and arms folded across his chest.

I glance at the bare desktop. "Yup. Just finished." Pride fills me.

"I see you and Gladys work well together." He pushes away from the wall and retrieves his coat from the closet, followed by mine. "You didn't find the work too boring?" He holds my coat open inviting me to put it on.

"Not at all. Organization is a hobby of mine." I slip into the warm, familiar embrace of dad's wool coat. "I enjoy a challenge."

"Of course, you do," he mutters, stepping away. "Shall we?"

I exit the suite first, and he locks the door behind us. In the elevator, I study his profile. The strong line of his jaw, those full kissable lips, the hint of a five o'clock shadow along his jaw. He's handsome. Classical silver screen handsome like Cary Grant or Mel Ferrer.

He glances at me out of the corner of his eye as the elevator slowly descends. "Are you hungry?"

"Starving," I confess dramatically. "I can make something when we get home. It's only fair."

"I have a better idea." A smile tugs at the corner of his mouth. "Would you like to get coffee first?"

"Starbucks?" My voice overflows with excitement. I've been craving a caramel macchiato since yesterday morning.

His brow furrows. "What's Starbucks?"

Shit. Oh, no. I broke the cardinal rule of time travel. No spoilers. "Nothing. Never mind."

"Is your memory coming back?" he asks as the doors slowly open on the ground floor. "You mentioned your coat belonging to your father this morning and now Starbucks. I can only assume these are familiar things to you."

"Snippets and flashes. I'm not sure how they all fit together yet," I lie.

"Well, I'll take that as a good sign." He opens the door for me, and we step out into the city shrouded in darkness and noise.

Cyril is waiting for us. He smiles when I rush toward the car. "Hello, Miss Kate. How was work?"

"Lovely, Cyril, thank you. I trust you had an uneventful day?"

"Always." He focuses on Arthur and sobers instantly. "Where to, boss?"

"Take us to the Red Maple, Jeeves."

Cyril glares at Arthur. The two men face off and I forget how to breathe. Are they going to fight?

"Yes, sir." Cyril opens the car door and helps me in.

Once the car weaves into traffic, Arthur relaxes beside me. I want to ask him why we're going there, but I sit quietly beside him and stare out the window. Everything looks so different and yet it's almost like nothing changed. The colorful characters who occupy the streets of New York are a bit more vibrant thanks to the preference for neon shades. But the hustle and bustle roars through the streets the same as it always has and always will.

The car rolls to a stop in front of a chrome and glass diner with a flashing red and white neon sign hanging over the door. The Red Maple. I remember Mom telling me about it, but I'd never been there. She once said they made the best pies in all five boroughs.

Arthur steps from the car and offers his hand. I take it feeling more like a spoiled princess than a temporary employee and uninvited houseguest. The warmth of his touch sends shivers of electricity coursing through my arm and directly into my chest. As soon as my feet are steady on the sidewalk, he releases me. Did he feel it too?

He escorts me inside where we take a booth in the corner next to a window giving us a view of the pedestrian traffic outside. Arthur sits with his back to the wall, his observant gaze flickering across the other patrons in the diner.

"How do you feel about pie?"

"I love pie." I settle back against the booth.

"What kind are you in the mood for?" He gestures to the glass case where a variety of choices await.

"Surprise me." Damn, this is reckless. I'm supposed to have amnesia and keeping track of my lies is becoming exponentially harder.

As I debate telling him the truth, a pretty waitress rocking Madonna's early signature look combined with her uniform sidles up to the table and lays two menus down.

"What can I getcha to drink?" She pops her gum and glances between us.

"Two coffees." Arthur slides the menus back toward her. "And two orders of apple pie a la mode."

The waitress scribbles down the order and retreats behind the counter.

Arthur leans back casually draping his arm across the seat. "How was your first day?"

"Great." I shift under the intensity of his gaze. "The work was pretty straight forward once I figured out the filing system."

"No problems otherwise?" He nods to the waitress who appears next to the table bearing two coffee mugs, creamer, and a steaming pot of coffee. After she fills both mugs, she leaves.

"No problems at all." I pull the mug closer and focus on adding some cream and sugar even though I normally only take a dash of milk.

"Do you have any questions?" He lifts his mug and sips the unadorned black coffee.

I stir my concoction and cringe when I taste how sweet it is. Shit. "About the job itself, no. I can't think of anything."

"My colleague, Mr. Cohen, will return to the office on Monday. You'll have a chance to meet him then."

My heart leaps at the thought and I smile at the prospect of seeing my father again. "I'm excited to meet him." I sip the coffee and choke it down. "Have you worked with your partners long?"

"Brooks and I have been together from the beginning. Cohen's only been with us for the past few years, but his work shows great skill and an eye for detail."

Hearing his high praise of my father's work makes me swell with pride. Dad had a talent for design. It surpassed most of the other architects of his time. Getting a position with this firm at the age of thirty proved to be the single greatest accomplishment of his short life.

The waitress appears again bearing our pie heaped with ice cream. "Enjoy."

I pick up my fork and take a bite. The buttery crust and sweet tang of apple filling melts in my mouth along with the decadent vanilla ice cream. The combination wrenches a moan from my throat.

Arthur pauses mid-bite and stares at me with an arched brow. "That good?"

"Better than sex," I murmur before stuffing another forkful into my mouth.

He chokes, and I meet his gaze across the table. In their stormy depths I see his hunger, and it has nothing to do with apple pie and coffee.

CHAPTER TEN

ARTHUR

"Better than sex."

The pie barely touches my tongue when her words strike me like a lightning bolt. I half-choke down the bite of now flavorless pie before meeting her innocent gaze. Maybe innocent isn't the right word, but I honestly don't know any other word to describe it. Those mesmerizing eyes widen with realization but no regret.

A volcanic heat rushes through my veins and a memory of her wearing skimpy lingerie flashes through my mind. Her tongue darts out to wet her lips before she presses them firmly together. It's becoming harder to deny this blossoming chemistry. Reckless, I dive headfirst into the flames.

"Perhaps you haven't found the right partner." I lift another piece of pie and grin at her dazed expression before consuming it.

Kate clears her throat and turns her reddening face away from me, focusing instead on the street outside. Her reflection in the glass betrays her reaction to my words. Her eyes drift closed for a brief moment. Her breath quickens. Her lips move silently, but I catch the way her teeth brush her lower lip when she mutters an unspoken curse.

I eat, patiently, calmly, waiting for her to regain some composure. Within moments she faces me again and picks up her fork. Kate and I resume our meal, ignoring the tension.

My words must have struck a chord, because her cheeks remain stained with a lovely blush until the last of the pie disappears from our plates. She sips the cold coffee and avoids making eye contact.

After I pay, we exit the diner and find Cyril waiting for us at the end of the block. The ride back to the apartment is painfully silent. I wonder if she's mulling over the possibilities of my response to her assessment of the pie. I am. I haven't stopped.

But questions remain. And until I have answers to those questions, I cannot indulge in what I truly want. No. Not yet. It is obvious Kate is keeping secrets, and I will uncover them through any means necessary.

Once we arrive at the apartment, Kate disappears in the bedroom, locking the door behind her. I pull off my jacket and jerk my tie free. Coming home to an empty apartment never bothered me before, but this week it became apparent something vital was absent for the past twenty years.

I turn on the TV desperate for some kind of distraction. MTV pops up on the screen in full annoying color. I'm more of a fan of the sixty's hits than this new shit. Most of it is loud and abrasive. I don't understand the fascination with heavy metal and hair bands. Even the pop racket grates on my nerves. But right now, I'm thankful for whatever distraction it provides.

A new video plays. I read the name of the band at the bottom. The Cars. The beat is catchy. It's not Elvis, but it works.

"Oh man, I love this song!" Kate steps from the bedroom wearing my plaid pajamas.

Suddenly, I wish I hadn't given her my clothes to wear. Her bare skin hidden beneath the thin layers of cotton fabric. I want to peel it off and explore every inch of her.

She sings along with the song completely oblivious to the wicked ideas crossing my mind. When she curls up on the couch beside me, my whole body tenses. I want to reach for her, drag her across my lap and taste her. I close my eyes and try to focus on anything besides this white-hot lust pulsing through me. So much for my plan to draw out her secrets.

Unless I use seduction. My cock pulses at the fleeting idea. No. I won't play that game. I can't. It wouldn't be fair to either of us.

"I haven't heard this song in so long." Kate leans back against the cushions and frowns. "It was one of my favorites as a kid. Dad loved The Cars."

Her confession makes me pause. "A kid?" I face her. "How old are you?"

A look of panic crosses her face. "A lady never reveals her age." She laughs. "I mean it makes me feel like a kid. My Dad loved all kinds of music. He got into their early stuff."

Kate shifts uncomfortably beside me. I'm not sure I believe her or not, but honestly, I may have misunderstood her. Since my cock's insistent demands distracted me.

"You like this crap?" I gesture toward the TV where a Michael Jackson video is blaring across the screen.

"Of course." She nods and remains focused on the TV. "Don't you?"

"No. I prefer Elvis, Bob Dylan, and Johnny Cash. Stuff I grew up with." I undo the top two buttons of my shirt.

She spins and scrunches up her face at me. "Bob Dylan? Seriously? I mean, his lyrics are iconic, but his voice...no, no way." Her gaze drops to where my hand at my throat.

"Doesn't mean I enjoy it any less." I shrug and work on my cufflinks.

"So, you don't enjoy any modern music?" Her voice cracks at the end as her curiosity keeps her attention fixed on my hands.

"Not really." I shrug. "My sister loves it. She works with all these people. I don't see the appeal."

"Wait? Marcy works with musicians?" Her jaw drops, revealing a beautiful row of pearly white teeth and a tongue I'd love to see put to good use.

"Musicians. Actors. Celebrities of all sorts. She's the most sought-after stylist in town." I steer my dirty thoughts back into neutral territory. "She didn't tell you?"

"No. I mean, she's stylish and knows her stuff," Kate sputters. "But she didn't give me any details or drop names."

Drop names? What the hell does that even mean? I push the question aside. "Yeah. After her divorce a few years ago, she got this great opportunity through one of the networks downtown and her business went through the roof."

Kate beams, and her smile hits me like a punch to the gut.

"That's amazing! It sounds like she's living the dream."

Living the dream. I marvel at the way she speaks. Her choice of words sometimes doesn't make sense without context. "Yeah, well, it used to be a nightmare."

Her smile faulters. "Her ex?"

"Yeah. The guy is an asshole. Rob and I tried to warn her, but she married him right out of high school." I dislike even thinking about it, but I keep talking unable to stop myself. "He controlled everything she did. Who she saw. Where she went. Hell, he even tried keeping her from visiting and calling her family."

"One of those guys." Kate nods solemnly. "I understand."

"When she finally caught him in bed with his co-worker's wife, she filed for a divorce." I ignore the emotions recounting this story brings to the surface. "I gave her a loan to get her on her feet. She refused to take a handout from anyone."

"Yeah, I would've been the same way." Kate props herself against the couch facing me. "You're a good brother, helping her when she needed it the most."

"She deserves the best, but she worked hard for what she has now." I chuckle at my sister's stubborn streak. "And she paid me back the full loan with interest. I'm proud of her."

Kate rests her hand on my shoulder. "Family is important. I don't have any siblings."

"Oh?" I ask, noting the shift in conversation. I press her further to see if her amnesia has finally lifted. "Were you close with your parents?"

She chews on her lip as she stares at the television. "Yeah. Dad died...a while back. Mom passed a few months ago. I miss them."

Interesting. I can't help but wonder if her memory recovered or if she even had amnesia to begin with. With the conversation so personal, I decide against calling her bluff and instead focus on drawing more out of her.

"Did you grow up in the city?" I ask, searching her profile.

Kate shifts her attention back to me and I note the panic etched deep in her mismatched eyes. "I think so." She laughs uncomfortably. "I don't remember exactly. The details are still kind of fuzzy."

"I understand. Rob did say the memories may be slow to return." I slowly rise to my feet. "I'm going to change."

"Oh, yeah. Of course."

"There's some leftover Chinese in the refrigerator if you're still hungry. The pie wasn't dinner. It's not nearly satisfying enough." I add the last part on a whim, teasing her. Another wave of blush stains her cheeks and she glances away.

"You're never going to let me forget I said that, are you?"

"Said what?" I shove my hands in my pockets. "Your assertion about pie being better than sex." Taking two steps backwards, I move closer to the bedroom. "Nope, probably not."

Inside the bedroom, I change into my pajama pants and an NYU sweatshirt. When I come back into the living room, Kate's in the kitchen heating up plates in the microwave. I hate the contraption and barely use it. She's bouncing around with the music on the TV.

Maybe I should call Rob and update him on her recovery. I slip into my drafting room and close the door. Of the two phonelines in the apartment, I rarely use this one, but this isn't a conversation I want to have in front of Kate.

After the fifth ring and no answer, I hang up and try the hospital number. The nurse transfers me to his line. Three rings and it connects.

"*Dr. Thompson.*"

"Rob, it's Arthur."

"*Hey, I meant to call yesterday, but the ER was chaos. How is your victim, I mean guest?*" Rob chuckles.

"Funny." I lean against the drafting table and lower my voice. "She's up and moving around. She went to work for me today."

"*You knock her out, take her home, and now she's your personal slave?*" Rob deadpans. "*No wonder you're a hit with the ladies.*" He clears his throat. "*Has she had any episodes of fainting, nausea, vomiting, or seizures?*"

"No."

"Is she eating? Drinking fluids? Resting?"

"Yes."

"Has her memory returned?" Rob asks methodically, running through a mental checklist.

"That's what I wanted to ask you. What should I expect? Will it all come back at once?" I don't mention her strange claims or the tidbits she's revealed about her family and her past.

"It depends. I've seen some patients where it comes back all at once. Sometimes it never comes back. And then there are others who seem to remember bits and pieces, but forget larger chunks of their memory." Rob exhales sharply. *"Has she mentioned anything about her past?"*

"A few details, but nothing giving me any idea who she is or where she came from." I tap my fingers on the desk.

"Damn. Well, don't push her too hard. Do you need me to stop by?" Rob shuffles some papers on his end of the line.

"No. I'll give you a call if anything changes."

"Sounds good."

"Have you found anyone looking for her at the local hospitals?" I ask, half-hoping he doesn't.

"No. Do you want me to put in a call to Richards down at the station, see if he can find anything to help us locate her family?"

"If you think it would help, yeah, but I don't have a lot of information to give him." Involving the police isn't ideal, but it's the last avenue to chase any possibilities.

"I'll give him a call after my shift. I need to run, some of us have lives to save."

"Thanks, Doc." My sarcasm earns me a brusque goodbye.

I rest my hand on the door and take a deep breath. Honestly, I shouldn't be this invested in someone I just met, but I can't help it. There's definitely something between us. I feel it. A gentle pull every time she walks into the room.

But there are too many unanswered questions, too many variables I have no control over. There is a reason I stay single and only casually date. I don't want complicated. I have no place for a wife or even a steady relationship.

Kate is most definitely a complication. She's worse than

that. She's a distraction. I have a firm to run. The last thing I need or want is a curvaceous hellcat tearing up my well-maintained life.

My fist taps against the wall repeatedly. It's like I have no control over my hormones when she's in the room. Even thinking about her pulls me deeper into fantasies I haven't allowed myself to indulge in—ever.

Yet, she rose to the challenge at the office today. Even though my schedule was full, I watched her carefully. She learns quickly and follows instructions to the letter. A strange sense of pride wells up deep in my chest. *Mine.*

No. I shake my head at the strange possessive thought. She's not mine. The irrational thought makes me recoil in horror. What would make me think such a thing?

The way she moaned while eating her pie. The way she so innocently claimed it was better than sex. The way my clothing caresses the sweet curves of her body. Her in my apartment. Naked in my shower. In my bed.

I pace the length of the room and rest my forehead against the cool glass of the window.

"Stop," I whisper to the voice in my mind telling me how easy it would be to seduce her, to lay claim to her.

You want her. You can't deny it.

I growl and my breath fogs the glass. No. Maybe I should ask Marcy if she can stay with her until she recovers. I can't ask Rob. That would be like feeding a lamb to a lion. It has to be Marcy. But I can't ask my sister to go out of her way because I'm uncomfortable. She has her own life and thriving business.

The memory of Kate lying unconscious on the floor outside my office haunts me. I did this to her. I hurt her. I can set this right. But I cannot concede to my baser desires.

Until Kate recovers, she is my responsibility, nothing more.

When I return to the living room, Kate is curled on her side, her head on my pillow, fast asleep.

My heart aches at the sight. I shove the tender emotions aside and pick her up. She nestles her face against my neck.

Fuck.

I carry her into the bedroom and lay her down on the bed. She sighs when I pull the blankets around her. Her sweet smile and bewitching eyes may be hidden from me, but they're burned into my memory.

Kate needs to get her memory back and fast, because if she doesn't, I don't know what I'm going to do. Part of me wants to crawl into bed beside her and hold her close. I can't shake the feeling this is exactly where she belongs, and that thought terrifies me more than anything.

CHAPTER ELEVEN
KATHERINE

After a long morning, I take my short lunch to retreat to the observation deck. The brisk air refreshes me and I feel closer to Dad than I have in years. It's Friday, which means in three days I'll finally get to see my father. Monday morning. I can hardly contain my excitement. I've waited this long, two more days should be no problem.

Less than a week into my new position and I've already fallen into a comfortable rhythm. Gladys helps me work through any issues and Arthur, while continuously busy, checks in periodically. There's definitely something to be said for the pace of the office setting without all the technology cluttering it up, but then again, I'd kill for a decent PC with a word processor over a typewriter.

The clear blue skies stretch for miles. Even though the sun shines brightly overhead, the air is crisp and cold. I pull my coat closer around me. Tourists bustle around the platform, but after living in the city for so long, I'm used to their presence. I lean against the railing where I stood only a few days ago contemplating the darkness around me. Today, there's a blossom of hope I never could have imagined.

I admire the city scape in the distance, but my attention always returns to the World Trade Center buildings. The constant visual reminder of my displacement in time leaves me uneasy. So many events take place during my lifetime, I never took the time to think about them before. Could I even influence major events and save lives? No, probably not.

Every book, movie, TV show featuring time travel I've ever seen shows the consequences of messing with past events. Then why am I here? If not to change the world, then to change my own destiny? Frustration overwhelms me.

I wish there were a handbook or an instruction manual to help me navigate time travel. I don't want to be the reason for nuclear war in the twenty-first century by accidentally stepping on a dragonfly. Ugh, the idea definitely leaves me queasy.

A glance at my watch tells me I should get back to work. Gladys wrote out a list of projects for me to tackle today. I'm glad for the challenge. I need something to occupy my thoughts. Between my excitement at seeing Dad next week and this complicated tension building with Arthur, my brain is overwhelmed.

The thought of Arthur makes my body heat. I push away from the railing and retreat into the elevator. Once I'm back inside the building, I unbutton my coat and refocus. This job may be temporary, but I'll do my damnedest to make sure it's done to the best of my ability.

I weave around a handful of people when I reach the fifty-fourth floor.

"Hi, Gladys. Did I miss anything?" I greet my co-worker as soon as I walk in the door.

Gladys jumps to her feet. "Oh, thank goodness you're back. Arthur wants you in his office the moment you return."

Fear grips me. What happened? What did I do? Did he somehow uncover the truth? I pull off my coat and hang it up.

"Did he say why?" I smooth my hands over my skirt.

She shakes her head. "No, but he's in there with Mr. Cohen right now. I'll let him know you're available."

Mr. Cohen. *Dad.* My heart stops. I'm not prepared. I'm not ready. Shit. Just breathe. I quickly adjust my blouse and pat my hair. Oh, God. I can't do this.

"Kate has returned, Mr. Maxwell." Gladys props the phone against her shoulder listening to his response. "Yes, sir. I will." She hangs up the phone and nods to me. "Go ahead in. They're waiting for you."

"Gladys, I..." My throat constricts.

"Don't worry. They won't bite. Go on, don't keep them waiting." She shoos me toward Arthur's office door.

I take several deep breaths before opening the door. Arthur glances up from behind his desk. He stands as I walk in and close the door behind me.

"You asked to see me, sir?" I keep my attention focused on him, but I can feel Dad's presence in the room. Those piercing eyes ground me. I take a breath and steady my racing heart.

"Yes, Kate. I want you to meet Victor Cohen, my associate." He turns away, and I follow his gaze. "Victor, this is my new assistant, Kate."

"Good to have you on board, Kate." Dad extends his hand and offers a sincere smile.

There's a stabbing pain in my chest from my heart exploding. I choke back a sob at the sight of him. His familiar mop of hair slicked back with precision, kind eyes, and commanding presence. He looks exactly like he does in the photograph I keep of him on my dresser. I want to scream and cry and throw myself into his arms, tell him how much I missed him. The desire to do it nearly overwhelms my sense. But I refrain.

Instead, I reach out and take his extended hand. "An honor, Mr. Cohen. I'm excited to work with you."

The heat of his hand engulfs mine. After thirty-two years of being deprived of his presence, his touch, I'm engulfed by a torrent of emotion by the simple contact. Pain, relief, joy, sadness, and every possible emotion in-between seems to catch me up in a hurricane. I may die, but it would be worth it for this one moment of reconnection. I shake his hand firmly and ignore my heart screaming inside my chest.

"Likewise." He releases me and steps back. His smile is kind and warm.

I clear my throat and smile turning back to Arthur. His expression is guarded and stern. I drop my gaze, unable to stand the intensity of the moment.

"Kate, would you please pull the file for the Mulligan Building as well as the Firehouse and Webber projects?" Arthur's deep voice reverberates off my soul.

I swallow the lump in my throat and meet his gaze. "Of

course." With a parting smile at Dad, I turn and leave the room.

Once I'm outside Arthur's office, I head directly for the filing cabinet and retrieve the files he requested. Staking them in a pile, I place them on Gladys's desk.

"Here are the files Mr. Maxwell requested." I gesture toward the door. "I need to use the ladies' room."

Gladys nods without glancing up from her typing. "Go ahead, dear."

The walls compress inwards. My head spins. I step out into the hallway and rush toward the restrooms located at the end of the corridor. Inside, it's empty. I collapse inside a stall and hang my head over the toilet as the nausea rolls over me. But nothing comes up and for once I'm glad I skipped lunch.

I slam the toilet seat down and collapse against the wall. Tears fall freely as the rush of emotions slam into me like a freight train.

How the hell can I do this? How can I work alongside Dad and not tell him the truth of my identity? How can I continue this charade with Arthur after all he's done for me? My heart splits with indecision. Even if I tell the truth, no one will believe me.

Arthur is a practical man. He won't believe I'm from the future. He'll think I'm insane and send me off to some asylum somewhere for psychiatric evaluation. Fear grips me. I'll never see Dad again. I'll be trapped here forever.

Too late. I'm already trapped here, in a time I don't belong. How is this even possible? I'm no closer to understanding how I got here than I am to understanding if there's even a way to get back to my time? I thump my head against the wall. Not that I want to go back to the future. The thought alone makes my skin crawl. I shiver. No. I'll make it work here, but I don't exist and this presents a problem.

At some point, I'm going to have to ask for help. The question is, who can I possibly trust with the truth of my situation? Another wave of nausea rolls over me and I wrap my arms around my waist.

What am I going to do? Maybe I should reach out to Marcy

or even Rob, the doctor friend of Arthur's. Deep in my mind, I know doing either would cause a rift between me and Arthur. If anything, I've learned Arthur is a fiercely loyal man, and while he may not understand my situation, he deserves the truth at some point.

I choke back a sob because I know the moment I tell him, whatever we have will be over. And the thought of losing him terrifies me more than the possibility of never seeing my parents again.

CHAPTER TWELVE
ARTHUR

I send everyone home early. Since it's Friday, no one questions my dismissal. It's been a while since I granted such a boon. Gladys beams at me when she exits the office reminding me to tell Kate when she returns from the restroom.

That won't be a problem because Kate is the very reason I'm sending everyone home early. After her unusual reaction to meeting Victor, the pieces are starting to fall into place. Finding Kate outside the office. Her questions about my associates, Victor in particular. But seeing her flustered response to his presence solidifies my suspicions.

What I hadn't anticipated was the surge of possessive jealousy to commandeer my common sense and rational thought. Jealousy because I want her to react to my presence. Possessive because Victor already has a beautiful wife. The undercurrent hums through me, and I pace my office unsure of how to even approach the conversation with Kate.

The outer office door closes. Kate's shadow falls across the frosted glass of my door.

After a deep breath to steel my expression, I open the door. The words die in my throat when I see Kate bent at the waist searching the bottom drawer of the filing cabinet. Her skirt rides high on the back of her thighs and all I can imagine is slipping my hand along those curves and baring her backside as she bends over my desk.

The filing cabinet slams shut.

I shake my head and clear my throat.

Kate snaps to attention, spinning around and pressing her hand against her chest. "You scared me."

"I apologize."

"Where did everyone go?" Kate asks glancing around the office.

"I gave them the rest of the day off." It's monumentally harder to gather my thoughts now since I've allowed my imagination to run free with that naughty fantasy. "Can I have a word with you in my office?"

Kate draws her lower lip between her teeth drawing my focus to her mouth. "Of course," she stammers before setting aside the files in her hand.

She looks nervous. Damn it. I didn't mean to make her uncomfortable, but she needs to understand. I need to understand.

Inside my office, Kate stands demurely with her fingers interlaced. "Did I do something wrong, sir?"

"Arthur." I lean against the desk in an attempt to make this conversation informal but still show the importance of its content. "When we're alone, call me Arthur."

She nods.

"Kate. I'm going to ask you a question, and I want you to be honest with me."

Her wide eyes flash with fear. "Okay."

"After I introduced you to my colleague, you seemed upset by the encounter." I tap my fingers on the edge of the desk. "What happened?"

Kate drops her gaze to the carpet. "It's nothing. I...well, he seemed familiar. The meeting must have triggered something in my memory." Her head shakes back and forth as she speaks.

"He reminds you of someone from your past?" My body tenses at the thought.

"That must be it." She shrugs her shoulders. "Although I still don't remember any details."

Disappointment settles over me, but I remain skeptical as to her designs on Victor. She doesn't seem like the type of woman who would set her cap on a married man. And yet I find myself addressing it with no qualms about my perspective.

"Victor came to tell me the good news." I straighten to my full height and shove my hands in my pockets. "He and his wife are expecting their first child. She's due in June."

"His wife. Pregnant." Kate sways but steadies herself on the back of the chair beside her. The color in her cheeks fades.

"Yes. They found out last week." I step closer.

"Last week." Kate pinches her eyes closed and nods slowly.

"Are you well?" I reach out and rest my hand on her shoulder. "You look like you're going to faint."

"I'm fine."

"Are you sure?" I pull her toward the chair. "Sit down. Do you need something to drink?"

"Yes, I'm sure." She waves her hand. "Don't worry about me."

"Kate." My voice is soft but firm. "Do you have any intentions of pursuing Victor?"

"Pursuing?" She stills and her bewitching gaze meets mine. "You think I'm attracted to Victor?"

I replay the memory her physical reaction to meeting Victor and her response to the news of his wife. "Yes. I do."

"What?" Her lips part in surprise. She covers her mouth and laughter fills the room.

"Why are you laughing?" I refrain from grasping her by the shoulders and demanding she explain herself. My hands clench into fists by my side.

"Because," she replies between peals of laughter. "You think I...Victor." Kate buries her face in her hands and her body shakes with mirth.

"When you're finished." I stare completely bewildered at why my comment would elicit such a response. "Please, take your time."

The sarcasm sobers her. "I'm sorry. It's, well, that's the most ridiculous thing I've ever heard."

I will never understand this woman. "I'm glad you find it amusing. Victor isn't only my colleague; he's my friend. I do not approve of flirtations, however innocent, with a married man."

"So, I can flirt with an unmarried man?" Kate's response comes with a smile.

Jealousy flares hot in my veins. "You cannot flirt with

anyone in my office. Period."

Rose blooms in her cheeks as she closes the gap between us. I stand my ground when she wraps her hand around my tie. Desire pulses around us, hot and desperate. She licks her tempting lips.

"Even you?" She tugs on the tie.

I grip her shoulders, keeping her from pulling me toward her. "I don't think this is a good idea."

"I agree. It could be an absolute disaster." She cocks her head. "I didn't ask for any of this, but here I am. We're in this together now. Why not make the best of it?"

"Kate." My reserve slips with the word. She's right. Heaven help me, she's absolutely right. I'm only a man. A man with needs and a willing woman in his arms. How long can I fight this magnetic pull? Reason begins to slip as she rises up on her toes.

"Arthur." She jerks on my tie, and I concede, closing the distance with a muttered curse.

Her mouth collides with mine, soft and pliant. I wrap my arms around her and deepen the kiss. She tastes like mint and lemon. Her curves press against my body teasing me with the innumerable possibilities. My hands wander along her spine until one cradles the back of her head and the other settles on her lower back. I want nothing more than to push her back on my desk and explore all of her.

Kate moans and flicks her tongue against mine. She runs her fingers through my hair, tugging and caressing. Soft breathy moans punctuate each kiss. My cock rubs against the zipper of my dress pants. She grinds her hips against me.

I break the kiss and hold her at an arm's length. "Kate. Wait."

Each breath is torture. I want to bury myself inside her. I want to taste her, commit her to memory, possess her completely. But I can't.

"We can't do this." I force myself to put up the barrier knowing my restraint is hanging by a few thin threads.

The passion in her eyes fades at my words. She straightens and steps away, her pained expression sends regret surging through me. I hate myself for ripping this moment from both of us, but it needs to be done.

"I'm sorry." I drop my hands to my sides. "Until your memory returns, I don't want to take advantage of you." Her stricken face makes his conscience twist.

"My memory might be gone, but I'm still able to decide what I want...and who." Kate pushes past me and pauses in the doorway. "Don't worry. I won't flirt with *anyone* in the office."

"Kate." I reach for her, but she's already gone.

Son of a bitch. I kick the trashcan and knock it over. What the hell did I just do? Raking my hand through my hair, I pace the office.

For years, I've been satisfied with my life. I never wanted a family, a wife or kids. Traditional expectations meant nothing to me. At least they didn't until I found myself at the end of my sanity over a curvy brunette with no memory of who she is or where she comes from.

I should drag her back into my office and show her exactly what she does to me, but I can't. I won't. And the damnedest part of it is...I can't think of a single, logical reason why I shouldn't.

CHAPTER THIRTEEN
KATHERINE

One week since the disastrous kiss, and I'm still not over it. Arthur locked himself in his studio the moment we got back to his apartment. He only came out to eat and use the bathroom, barely sparing me more than two words every time he emerged from his dungeon over the weekend.

I stole an empty notebook from the drawer in the closet and spent my copious amounts of free time writing while the television played in the background. I had no other way to document my thoughts since there was no one I could trust with the truth.

Over two days, I poured my heart and soul into the notebook, documenting everything from the events of the past year to my conflicting emotions for Arthur. Part of me hoped I could somehow make sense of what was happening, but my words sound like the rantings of a lunatic. I sincerely doubt there would ever be anyone who would understand and not want to ship me off to a shrink.

Come Monday morning, we were back on speaking terms. I wanted to talk to him about what happened in his office last Friday, but the stern expression and steely determination in his eyes warned me of another week of silent treatment should I pursue the subject.

Then I saw Dad. We formed a fast friendship right away, and he asked for my opinion several times over the next few days. I did what I could to help. It felt so good to spend time with him.

I tried not to stare or seek him out. After what Arthur insinuated last week, I did my best to contain my emotions around my father. Last thing I wanted was a misunderstanding, awkward as that would be. I wasn't here to make trouble. A second chance dropped into my lap, and I am determined to enjoy all of it.

"Kate, I need you to take a letter for me," Arthur calls from his open office.

Wrapped in nerves and anticipation, I grab my notepad and join him. When I walk into his office, I remember how his lips tasted, how hard he was for me. How he pushed me away. Taking the seat across from his, I'm keenly aware of his presence. I poise the pen over the paper.

"Ready." I refuse to look up. If I meet his gaze right now, I may combust.

At his silence, I glance up to see if he heard me. His stare pins me to the leather chair, and I shift uncomfortably under his scrutiny. Then, as if nothing were amiss, he launches into dictating the letter.

I write quickly, but he slows enough for me to keep up. I wish I could type it in Word directly. My typing skills are faster than my makeshift shorthand. Another downside to the eighties, I guess.

When he finishes, I stand, ready to retreat back to my desk. The resignation in his voice stops me.

"Kate, you don't have to run away from me."

"I'm not running." I fold my arms across my chest shielding my heart with the legal pad. "I have work to do, as do you."

He scoffs but shakes it off. "Have you finished organizing the projects for the promotional packet I requested?"

"I'll have it for you by the end of the day." I tap my fingers on the pad. "Anything else I can do for you?"

The tick in his jaw is prominent even from ten feet away. He wants me to remain professional, and I will. Even if my whole body screams for his attention. I want his mouth on me again. I want more than I should and knowing I affect him as much as he affects me has my willpower burning to ash.

"No, that will be all." He clears his throat. "Type this letter up for me to sign and then mail it before the end of the day."

I nod, swallowing my disappointment, and retreat to my desk. As I begin to type the letter, Gladys waves from across the room. I stop clicking on the keys and return the gesture.

Within moments, she's by my side. I pause midway through the letter.

"Did you hear the news?" Gladys squeals with excitement.

"What news?" I ask. Her energy seeps into me dispelling the lull left in the wake of my interaction with Arthur.

"Mr. Cohen's wife is going to have a baby!" She dances around in a tiny circle. "Oh, I'm so excited for them."

"That's wonderful." I choke out the words with a fake smile while my mind spins. *Pregnant with me. My mom, pregnant with me.* The whole situation is trippy as fuck.

"I found out while you were in the office with Mr. Maxwell. She told me the good news herself!" Gladys snatches a butterscotch candy from the bowl on my desk and unwraps it.

"Wait." The room spins like a carnival ride, and I grip the chair to keep me steady. "She's here. Now?"

Gladys pops the candy in her mouth and nods. "She's in her husband's office now. Brought him an afternoon snack. Isn't she sweet? Those two are adorable together." She sighs dramatically. "I hope I can find a love like theirs one day."

My heart twists in my chest, pounding so loud I hear the repetitive beat pulsing in my skull. I stare at the door to Dad's office. Two shadows move beyond the tinted glass. My parents. Behind that door. Together. I press my hand over my heart and breathe deep.

"You okay? You're a little flushed?" Gladys eyes me with concern.

"Fine. Just heartburn. Lunch was too spicy I think." I brush it off with little effort.

"I have some Alka Seltzer in my purse, if you need it."

"I'll be fine. Thanks though, I appreciate it." I smile. "I should finish this. Needs to go out today."

Gladys nods. "Don't work too hard. No reason to let him work you into the ground."

Once she retreats, I focus on the letter. But my mind drifts back to the office where I know my parents are talking. On the last line, I type out Arthur's name and leave room for a signature before reading through the letter for any errors. As I pull it from the machine, Dad's office door opens.

"Don't forget to stop by the bank on the way home." Mom's voice drifts through the room and I'm transported through the past thirty odd years of my life.

"Oh, you're here. Good." Dad comes up to the desk with his arm around Mom's waist. "Kate, I'd like you to meet my wife, Nora." He radiates love as he gazes at Mom. "Honey, this is our new secretary, Kate."

Mom holds her hand out. "Lovely to meet you, Kate."

I want to burst into tears. But even more, I want to launch myself across this desk and hug her. God, I miss her so much. I swallow the emotions clawing at my chest screaming for release. My gaze drifts between my parents and I muffle a sob behind a gentle cough before taking her hand.

"Nice to meet you as well."

Mom looks the same as I remember even though she's younger than I've ever seen her, except for photographs. Her dark hair holds no trace of gray and no worry lines mar her fair skin. She's positively glowing. Even beneath the flowing fabric of her gown, I note the soft curve of her stomach.

"Kate. Is that short for Katherine?" Mom muses tapping her finger on her chin.

"Yes, it is." The words spring from my lips without hesitation.

"It's so elegant." She laughs. "I'll add it to the list of possible girl names. What do you think, Victor?"

"I like it." He grins. "Very classy."

"You're having a baby?" I play it off wanting a bit more time with both of them, together.

"Yes. Our first."

"Congratulations." I force a smile remembering the stories Mom told me about how lucky they were to have me. I was her little miracle. "That's wonderful news."

Her hand rests protectively over her stomach. "We're extremely fortunate. Our little miracle."

My heart aches at the words I heard so often over the years.

Tears form at the corner of my eyes and I blink furiously in a vain attempt to stop them.

"Arthur, there you are." Mom turns away, thankfully missing my emotional display.

I dash the tears away with my sleeve and swallow hard while their attention shifts to Arthur.

"Nora. You look radiant." Arthur hugs Mom and places a kiss on her cheek. "Did you get the flowers I sent?"

She slaps his shoulder playfully. "You charmer. I don't know why you sent me such an ostentatious bouquet."

"You didn't like it?" He frowns.

"She loved it," Victor adds. "Don't let her modesty fool you."

"How did you know my favorite flowers were peonies?" Mom teases him. "Did you ask Victor for help picking them out?"

"Actually, I chose them at Kate's suggestion." He steps closer and rests his hand on the back of my chair. "She's very detail oriented."

The compliment melts over me and I stare at Arthur in shock.

"You have wonderful taste, Kate." She grins. "I think we're going to be good friends."

Oh, Mom. "I think so too."

No matter how much I want this moment to last, how much I want my parents wrapped in a protective shield to be happy and together forever, reality lingers in the back of my mind hovering like a storm building a dangerous momentum.

"Well, I should get home." Mom waves. "I enjoyed meeting you, Kate. We'll talk again soon."

"I'd love that," I reply as Dad leads her to the exit.

"Is the letter ready yet?" Arthur's voice startles me.

I hold the paper up, bitter at his ability to ruin the moment. "Yes."

He takes the letter and leans down until his breath brushes my ear. "Is my portfolio ready?"

My fingernails dig into my palms. If I turn my head, I could easily press my lips to his. I could take what I want. But I don't. He's toying with me now. Testing me. I refuse to play his game.

"Is the day over?" I snap under my breath.

"I want it on my desk by five." His voice burrows beneath my skin infusing me with heat.

"Yes, sir." I couldn't stop the sarcastic bite to my words.

"Don't test my patience, Kate," he growls.

I close my eyes and the heat of him disappears. When I spin around, his door closes with a forceful thud.

Whatever battle began last week, Arthur seems determined to win at all costs. Is he trying to break me? Trying to get me to admit something?

I have no idea what his problem is, but if he persists, I'll have no choice but to call his bluff.

Victor saunters back into the office and knocks on my desk. He's beaming with optimism, bouncing on the balls of his feet. "Smile, Kate. It's a good day to be alive."

His grin infects me with hope. "Yes, it is."

Once he disappears in his office, I slump in my chair. I should be happy for my parents, but I know what's coming. All I can do is pray I haven't caused a fracture in the space-time continuum or a paradox or some insane butterfly effect.

Pushing the existential crisis aside, I focus instead on finishing the portfolio for Arthur. The insufferable ass won't let me hear the end of it if I don't meet my deadline. I will not let him win.

Not this round.

CHAPTER FOURTEEN

ARTHUR

The moment I close the door to my apartment, the infuriating woman cloisters herself away in my bedroom. The only words she spared during the ride home after work were directed at Cyril. She treated me like I wasn't even there. Each passing moment grew heavier with the weight of our silence.

Part of me wanted to grab her by the shoulders and kiss some sense into her. I swore to show some restraint. One of us needs to act with some sense.

She claimed she had no romantic interest in Victor, but I saw the way they interacted at the office. All week they worked together, laughing and talking. I wanted to say something, but their actions never broached the boundaries of propriety. No one would even suspect Kate and Victor of crossing that line. And yet, like an insatiable itch, it festered in my mind.

When I saw her talking with Victor and Nora, my curiosity commandeered any rational thought. Even though she thought no one noticed, I saw the shift. The sadness beneath the smiles. There was something there, and Kate was determined to hide it from the world. From me.

Over the last week, I did my best to give her a wide berth. The kiss seared me like a brand. Every time I close my eyes, I can feel her in my arms, taste her on my tongue. She wants me, just as I want her. But it doesn't feel right. With her still recovering her memories, I would only be taking advantage of her vulnerability. At least that's what I tell myself.

What if she's already taken? She said she wasn't married, but that doesn't mean she's not in a relationship with someone. The thought haunts me. I can't admit it aloud, and I'm terrified to ask for fear it may trigger a memory.

But we can't avoid each other indefinitely. There needs to

be a compromise if we're stuck together.

I cross the room and knock on the door. "Kate. We need to talk."

She opens the door and I'm distracted by the skin tight leggings and a loose sweatshirt draped precariously low on one side baring the creamy expanse of her shoulder. Kate eyes me as she pushes past, heading directly for the kitchen.

"Goddamn it. Kate, you can't ignore me forever." I follow trying not to catch a glimpse of her ass when she bends over to grab a bottle of wine from the refrigerator.

"I'm pretty sure I can." She spins around and grabs the corkscrew off the counter beside me before heading for the living room.

With a muttered curse, I find her curled on the couch drinking directly from the bottle.

"How classy." I cross my arms and shake my head. "Would you like a glass?"

Bold as gilded lettering, Kate meets my gaze and swigs from the bottle.

"Very mature." I'm two seconds from snatching her off the couch and bending her over my lap.

She ignores me and turns on the television with the remote. Music fills the room. Her attention fixes on the screen behind me.

"At some point, you're going to have to talk to me." I stand directly between her and the television.

Kate licks her lips and her glare sends a shiver of need straight to my cock. Pliant Kate may be attractive, but feisty Kate is sure to bring a whole new dimension to the bedroom.

I shake the inappropriate thoughts from my mind. "Must you behave like a child?"

"How would you like me to behave, Arthur?" The emphasis she places on my name sets my teeth on edge.

As I open my mouth to respond, the phone rings. I snatch it from the receiver. "What?" I snap.

"Easy there, Arthur. I need you to buzz me in." Marcy has the damnedest timing, but honestly, I'm thankful for the reprieve. Maybe Kate will open up to my sister if she won't talk to me.

"Fine." I hang up and hit the button on the panel near the door.

Kate's drowning in chardonnay in front of the television, so she doesn't even notice when Marcy arrives.

I pull her aside out of view of Kate the moment she walks in the door. "What the—"

"I need you to do me a favor."

"Oh, another favor? Does this earn me Mom's crystal vase?" Her eyes glitter.

"You're a heartless vulture, you know?" I sigh. "Fine."

"What do you want me to do?" she asks, popping her gum.

"I want you to hang out with Kate tonight. See if you can get her to open up."

"Hang out with Kate?" Marcy laughs. "I was planning on doing that anyway. Would've done it for free."

"I hate you."

"You love me." She grins. "Wait, has her memory come back?"

I run my hand through my hair. "Honestly, I have no fucking idea. She won't talk to me, and I'm about to strangle her."

Marcy's smile widens. "What happened? You two fuck?"

"No. We didn't fuck." I tip my head back and stare at the ceiling. "We kissed last week."

"No way." Marcy shoves me. "About time you showed some interest in someone who isn't a goddamn brainless mannequin."

"What do you know? You spent all of what, an hour with her last week?"

"And you're an expert on the female mind?" Marcy laughs. "Well, whatever happened. I'm glad. You needed your orderly existence disrupted."

"I don't think she's being honest with me. Some of her memories seem to be coming back, but I can't shake this feeling there's more she's not telling me." I glance around the corner.

Kate's riveted by whatever's on the screen.

"I doubt she's plotting anything nefarious." My sister pats me on the shoulder in a sad effort to placate me. "But I'll sacrifice my Friday night to sit on the couch, drink wine, and gossip, if it will ease your conscience."

When she phrases it like that, it sounds ridiculous, but I'm already committed to this plan. "Fine."

"Good. Why don't you go out? Call Rob. Hit the bar." She cocks her head at my hesitant expression. "I can't work my magic with you here, Arthur. Go."

"Okay." I square my shoulders and head back into the living room. "I'm going out."

Marcy pops around the corner, and Kate's scowl transforms into a brilliant smile.

"Marcy! What are you doing here?"

"I thought I'd come over and we could spend some quality time together." Marcy turns and shoos me with her hand. "Go. Out with you. Girls' night."

I roll my eyes when she collapses on the couch next to Kate and grabs the bottle. If anyone can help me now, it's Marcy. She may seem flighty and eclectic, but I trust her with my life.

Their laughter fills the room. They don't even notice when I walk past them. Once I'm in the hallway, I push aside any hesitancy at leaving Marcy alone with Kate and press the button for the elevator.

Rob lives on the twenty-third floor of the same building, which can be both a curse and a blessing. I hesitate before aggressively pressing the doorbell outside his apartment.

I'm shocked when the door swings open, and Rob fills the doorway wearing a robe over his t-shirt and sweatpants. "Arthur? What the hell are you doing here?"

I push past him and head right for his stash of booze. "Marcy came over to keep Kate company." I pop the lid off the scotch and pour it in a glass.

"Let me guess, you weren't invited to their little pajama party?" he says leaning against the bar beside me.

"Nope." I down the shot without a second thought.

"Well, I'm glad you came." Rob saunters over to the dining room table and picks up a thin manila folder. "Richards came by the hospital today and gave me this."

I take the folder and flip it open. Inside is one sheet of paper. I read it and toss the paper back in the folder. "What the fuck does this mean?"

"Your mystery woman." He pours himself a scotch and lifts it in salute. "She doesn't exist."

I scoff. "What the fuck do you mean she doesn't exist? She's sitting in my apartment right now."

"I don't know what to tell you." He shrugs. "I gave a description and all the information you provided. Richards says there's nothing. No missing person's file fitting her description. Nothing."

I toss the file aside. "Bullshit. She's as real as you and me."

"I know." He pours two more shots. "It doesn't make any sense, does it?"

"Someone has to know who she is?"

"Cheers." Rob lifts his glass in salute.

Raising my glass, I drift off into my own mind. If there's no record of her and no missing person's report, then who the hell is she? How the hell did she end up in my lap? I toss the alcohol down my throat and grimace at the burn.

"What are you going to do?" Rob asks eyeing me with interest.

"What do you mean?" The alcohol doesn't sit well. I tap my chest with my fist.

"She can't stay with you indefinitely." Rob leans against the bar.

"Well, she's working for me for the moment." I shrug. "I guess we'll have to find a place for her somewhere besides my apartment."

"Yeah, sure." Rob laughs. "You can't fool me."

"Fool you about what?"

Rob stares at me like I've sprouted a horn in the center of my forehead. "In twenty-some years of friendship, I've never seen you this worked up over a woman."

I pour another shot. "I'm not worked up over anything."

"Yes, you are." Rob moves the bottle out of reach. "Listen. You can't kick her out. She has nowhere to go."

I down the liquor and immediately regret it. "I missed the part where that's my problem." Before he can remind me how I assaulted her, however accidental it was, I continue. "She may not have recovered all her memory, but she's perfectly capable of fending for herself. I gave her a job, which provides a lifetime worth of torture on a daily basis. I don't need her fucking up my personal life too."

"What personal life?" he scoffs. "All I'm saying is, it sounds like you two need to fuck and get it out of your system."

"Yes. Sex will obviously solve all my problems. Perhaps her memory will magically return afterwards." I tap the glass on the bar. "Then I can get her off my hands."

"I'm used to you being an asshole, but this is overboard even for you." He snatches the glass from my fingertips and walks around the bar. "What gives?"

I hang my head. "I wish I knew. This woman has me all twisted up. The moment I think we're on solid ground everything gives out beneath me and can't tell which end is up."

He offers a glass of water. I sip it wondering if I can even voice my concern out loud and not sound like a raging lunatic.

"I can smell the smoke from the gears spinning in your head." He sips his water. "Just say it."

"I don't think she has amnesia." I stare into the glass. "She's not being honest with me."

"What makes you say that?" Rob straightens and sets the drink aside.

"The way she talks. The way she interacts with people. With me." I shake my head. "I don't know how to explain it, but it's like she has this carefully constructed persona and every now and then she'll say or do something that doesn't make sense. I don't know."

"Have you asked her about it?"

"No."

"You should."

"Why? What good is asking about it?" I rub my forehead. "She'll only deny it."

Rob throws his hands up. "All I know is it wouldn't hurt for you two to talk about it, you know, like adults."

I cock my head and pin him with a disappointed glare. "Yes, because behaving like honest adults has worked so well for you and Marcy."

"Don't bring us into your shitshow." He gestures between us. "I'll talk to Marcy when I'm good and ready."

"Better hurry, the window of opportunity narrows with every date she goes on." I click my tongue. "Gotta catch her before she realizes she's better off alone."

"I'm not discussing this with you." Rob rinses his hands and pats them dry. "Let's go. We're going to crash the pajama party so I don't have to deal with your miserable ass all night."

I can't believe this man has been my best friend for as long as he has. I should have killed him long ago. I hate when he's right.

My stomach lurches at the prospect of confronting Kate, but the nausea doubles when I think about Marcy and Rob together. That's a visual I didn't need.

CHAPTER FIFTEEN
KATHERINE

Halfway through the second bottle of wine, Arthur fades into the back of my mind. Marcy and I watch MTV while she tells me spills all the delicious gossip about working backstage with all the celebrities.

It's so difficult not to say anything. I catch myself a few times nearly spilling spoilers for the next thirty-five years. Having this kind of foreknowledge is a curse.

As she tells her stories, I listen intently asking questions and finding ways of relating to the conversation.

"Oh, there are some tasty stories about that man, let me tell you." She launches into an encounter she had with one of the most prominent men in New York. I bite my tongue because...spoilers.

We finish the bottle of wine, and Marcy volunteers to get a new one from the kitchen. She pops the cork and pouts. "Arthur should really invest in a better wine selection."

"I don't know. This stuff isn't bad." I sip the red wine. It's drier than I would normally drink, but overall, it's good.

Marcy scoffs. "My brother has great taste in everything except wine and women."

Her words strike my own insecurities. "Why do you say that?"

"His prior string of girlfriends were complete idiots. Pretty faces with empty heads." She sticks her tongue out in disgust. "I mean, I get it. He's focused on his career. His buildings are his children, so he's not interested in tying himself down to a real family."

Disappointment tugs at my conscience, which I shove away.

"It's sad, really. To see him so successful and yet at the end of the day, he has no one to share it with." She swirls the wine in the glass and shrugs.

"He has you." I counter. "And Rob."

Marcy tilts her head and fixes her blue shadowed gaze on me. "It's not the same as having a loving wife, maybe some kids." She sighs. "I shouldn't talk. After my shitty marriage ended in flames, you would think I'd be against the whole institution."

"I understand the feeling." The alcohol loosens my inhibitions, but with Marcy, I find it so much easier to forget the reality of my situation. "My ex broke up with me three weeks before Christmas."

"Wow. What an asshole." Marcy shakes her head.

"Yeah. I mean, it had been over for a while, but I had so much invested in him and kept hoping it would get better." The memories assault me, and I bat them away angrily. "It never did."

"Yeah. Sounds like my ex." She raises her glass in a toast. "To new beginnings. Fuck those boys who couldn't handle how awesome we are."

"I'll drink to that." I drink deeply. "This year is already shaping up to be better than the last, although that doesn't mean much. Last year was hell." I tick the reasons off on my fingers. "I lost my job, my mom died, and asshole left me high and dry." A harsh laugh escapes. "I should be thankful for the last one though."

"Oh honey." Marcy rests her hand on my knee. "I'm so sorry about your mom."

"She'd been sick for a while." My voice cracks. "We knew she didn't have much time left. But damn it all if life had to kick me at my weakest moment."

"That's the worst. Come here. You need a hug." Marcy embraces me.

I relax against her, the scent of Aquanet tickles my nose and tugs at my memories. I can almost picture mom holding me close, telling me it'll work out in the end. The brutal pain of the last year slowly ebbs into acceptance. It feels good to vent and get it off my chest. I didn't realize how much I missed having someone to talk to and trust.

When we break apart, she fills our glasses. "So, I have to

know. What is going on with you and Arthur? He seemed a little pissy earlier."

I wave my hand. "Honestly, I don't know. One minute he's distant, the next he's thoughtful and kind."

"Sounds like Arthur." Marcy heaves a dramatic sigh. "He wouldn't recognize a good thing if it slapped him in the face." She grins. "I guess I'll take it as a good sign he hasn't kicked you out of his apartment yet."

"What do you mean?"

"He never lets anyone stay here. Even when I separated from my ex, he didn't offer to let me stay with him." She chuckles. "Not like I would have. He's impossible to live with, and I'm much too free-spirited to share a space with a control freak."

Her admission hits me square in the chest and steals my breath. "He's only doing it because he feels guilty for knocking me out."

"Yes, that's probably true. Or it was in the beginning." She props her elbow on the back of the couch and leans her head on her hand. "I almost offered to let you stay with me, but seeing him all twisted up and tripping over himself over having to take care of someone other than himself, well, it's good for him to step outside his own perfect box once in a while."

A snort-laugh escapes before I can stop it. I clap my hand over my mouth.

"I'm an evil genius, I know." She winks. "I half-hoped he'd be in love with you by now."

"We met last week!" I gape at her. "You didn't know anything about me."

"Honey, it's my job to be able to read a client's personality and find their perfect fit. This extends to matchmaking." She laughs at the stunned expression on my face. "Chemistry, baby. That's all it is. When you try on a dress and its instant love, the same thing applies to people."

I snap my jaw closed. "I'm not sure whether to be horrified or impressed by your confidence." She's right about the chemistry between us, but Arthur overcoming whatever hurdle he's erected between us has proved to be damned irritating.

"He's being stubborn, isn't he?" Marcy groans.

"Yes." I finish the wine and set the glass aside. "After we kissed, it's like he's actively trying to keep me as far from him as he can."

"You kissed?" Marcy damn near spills her wine. "When the hell did this happen?"

Heat rises in my cheeks. "A week ago."

"Hah! Chemistry." She punches the air with her bangled fist. "Told you."

"It only made things worse." I hang my head. "The only time he's ever around me is when I'm talking with someone else."

"Is this with anyone else or only other men?"

"Anyone, really." I think about the past week. "If I didn't know any better, I would think he's possessive, but honestly, he probably doesn't trust me."

"He doesn't trust anyone." Marcy taps her manicured fingernails against her lips. "But this is more than that for sure."

Before I can even ponder her words, Rob and Arthur appear in the doorway. Rob hangs back, his gaze appraising as it skims over me and lingers on Marcy.

"Sorry to interrupt the party, ladies." Rob and Arthur share a look.

Arthur's stiff posture and the gentle clench and release of his fists by his side betray the tension radiating from him. He seems uncomfortable, and that's putting it mildly.

"No problem." Marcy jumps to her feet. "Want something to drink, Rob? Come to the kitchen."

I know what she's doing and she's not even trying to hide it. Rob joins her in the kitchen. Even though it's open to the rest of the apartment, there's a shift in energy with Arthur and I remaining in the living room.

"You should find your own place." Arthur's statement cuts straight through the tension stealing all the warmth from the room.

What little confidence I gained from my conversation with

Marcy pops like a bubble. My chest constricts under the intensity of his gaze. He remains firm.

A scuffle of commotion in the kitchen behind me brings me to my senses. "Yeah, you're right."

When I stand up, I grip the sofa to keep from falling. Three bottles of wine hit me at once.

In a flash, Arthur's across the room and catches my elbow. I jerk out of his grasp. "No. You don't get to play hero, Arthur. You want me to leave. I'll go."

"I didn't mean right this second." His voice grates against my mind creating friction and heat. "You're drunk. I'll help you find a place tomorrow."

"No." I stumble back out of his reach. The tenuous connection we have pulls tight, a fraying thread barely holding. "You've done enough."

Arthur roughly runs his hand over his face and through his hair. "Damn it, Kate."

The biting edge of his words cuts the final tether. An alcohol induced haze filters through my reason. My heart plunges to the pit of my stomach and bile burns the back of my throat.

I race past him stumbling around the furniture. He reaches out and grabs my wrist.

"Kate. I want you to be honest with me."

My stomach churns and I shake my head. "No. You don't."

I wrench myself out of his grip and dart into the bedroom. By the time I reach the bathroom, it's too late. I double over the toilet heaving as my body purges the copious amounts of wine I drank.

Tears sting my eyes as my stomach heaves. My body shakes. Stupid. So stupid. My hand grips the toilet.

"Easy now," a man's gentle voice echoes behind me. It's not Arthur, it's Rob. He gathers my hair in his hand and rubs a cool cloth against the back of my neck. "Better get it all out."

Mortified, I pinch my eyes closed wishing I were still in my present. No matter what the decade, I am still a hopeless disaster.

"Leave." I try to shoo him away.

"Nice try, Kate." Rob's soft chuckle echoes off the tile. "I'm a doctor. A little vomit doesn't scare me."

My stomach heaves again. I want the ground to open up and swallow me, put me out of my misery.

Arthur wants me to be honest with him, but I know the truth will do nothing but drive a deeper wedge between us. Maybe that's better than lying. No one would believe me anyway.

CHAPTER SIXTEEN
ARTHUR

The bathroom door slams from inside the bedroom making me grit my teeth. What the fuck did I do? Kate looked ready to shatter into a thousand delicate pieces. I knew the moment I opened my mouth, something bad would happen.

"You're an asshole!" Marcy charges from the kitchen after breaking free from Rob's hold.

I brace myself for impact. She's got a mean right hook and isn't afraid to use it. But instead of lunging at me, she heads for the bedroom to help Kate.

Rob catches up to her and they exchange a few muffled, heated words. Marcy nods and crosses her arms, spinning around to face me, while Rob ventures into the bedroom after Kate.

I swallow the jealousy raging deep inside me. I can't go after her, not after what I said. What I did. Marcy's right, I am an asshole.

"What the hell was that about?" Marcy lays into me. She's a good six inches shorter and half my weight, but I hate being on the receiving end of my sister's wrath.

"What?" I shrug as though it doesn't bother me, but it does. It tears me apart. "She can't stay here any longer. I did my part. I even gave her a job. End of story."

"You're a goddamn saint." She glowers. "Do you want a fucking award for being a decent human being?"

"No. I just want my life back."

"Yeah. It's such a charming existence living in your penthouse all alone." She spits venom. "I was right, you wouldn't know a good thing if it fell out of the sky and danced in your lap."

"What the hell is that supposed to mean?" I snap.

"Kate." Marcy says her name like it's the answer to the

ultimate question of the universe.

"I've known her for less than two weeks." I gesture toward the bedroom where she and Rob are locked in the bathroom. "She doesn't even know who she is."

"Has it ever occurred to you she knows who she is but decided not to tell you because it's none of your goddamn business?" Marcy stalks closer and jabs a finger in my chest.

Her words stun me for a moment, but I focus on the first part of the question rather than the later. "Yes. I had a feeling she lied to me from the very beginning about having amnesia."

"And yet you didn't ask her directly?"

"I tried." I exhale growing exhausted. "When I ask, she hedges around it."

"What if it's painful for her to think about her past? Did you ever think about that?" Marcy's eyes flash with anger and unshed tears. "Did you ever think maybe she was like me? Trying to break free from a horrible, inescapable situation? Not everyone has someone to come to their rescue, to give them a chance to start over."

Goddamn it. My mood takes a nosedive into misery. "No. I didn't even think of that."

"Of course not. Who would? You live up here in your gilded penthouse with everything you could ever want and no one to challenge you." She wipes the tears with the sleeve of her shirt leaving tearstains on the neon fabric.

"Marcy." I reach for her, but she steps back and shakes her head rapidly.

"No. I'm not the one you should apologize to. I'm not the one you strung along and then kicked to the curb."

Indignance rises up to defend me. "I didn't string her along. We kissed once. It was a mistake, and I told her I had no intention of pursuing anything further between us."

"You think it matters?" Marcy laughs. "The tension between you two is so thick I could cut it with shears. You can deny it all you want to, big brother, but the sparks flying between you two don't lie."

"I don't need a relationship." Even the words sound weak

when I speak them aloud. "I don't want one. I'm happy with my life."

"Not everything is about you, Arthur."

"I helped her out, gave her a place to stay. Hell, I'll even help her find a place and get a permanent job."

"And then what? You'll both go your separate ways and live happily ever after."

"Something like that."

"Where did you find her?" Marcy's voice softens a fraction. "New Year's Day."

"What's that have to do with this?" I'm confused by the shift in the conversation.

"The guard said he saw her on the observation deck, didn't he?" Marcy continues. "Before you conked her on the head with the door outside your office."

My eyes drift closed. "No. That can't be right."

"A lot of desperate people have taken the jump." Marcy shrugs. "From what she told me, last year was a hell of a struggle. Desperation makes us do crazy things."

"But she didn't jump. I found her outside my office." I reason. "Why come to the fifty-fourth floor?"

"Maybe you should ask her."

"She won't tell me." I swallow my pride for a moment.

"You're asking her to be honest with you, when you can't even be honest with yourself." My sister rests her hand on my arm and squeezes. "You feel something for her and it scares the ever-loving shit out of you."

The sincerity of her words sends a bolt of realization straight through my heart. I shake my head, unable to think or even speak.

"I love you, Arthur. You came to my defense when no one else would." Her soft tone makes my heart ache. "I want you to be happy, and you can't be happy until you face the truth. One day you're going to wake up alone and realize you let *the one* get away."

Unable or unwilling to face the reality of her words, I turn away. Halfway to the door, Marcy's voice stops me.

"Don't be an idiot!"

Without hesitation, I stalk toward the door, grab my coat from the rack, and head out into the night. I need to think, so I retreat to the one place where I know I can clear my head. The observation deck of the Empire State Building.

Out in the cold, January night, I bundle myself deeper in my wool coat. It seems even in trying to escape facing Kate, I run directly into her arms by putting myself in her exact position.

Marcy may have a point, but I'd rather die than admit it to her.

CHAPTER SEVENTEEN
KATHERINE

After a hot shower and a warm cup of peppermint tea, I feel almost human. Exhausted, both physically and emotionally, yes, but Rob and Marcy make sure I have everything I need. With the alcohol purged from my system, all I want is sleep.

Once I'm tucked in a warm pair of oversized pajamas and snuggled beneath the soft warm sheets, it hits me. Arthur wants me to leave. I try to protest and climb from the bed, but Marcy gently pushes me back. I'm too weak to fight.

"Rest," Marcy instructs in her most maternal voice.

"Arthur said..." I lick my lips as the words trail off.

"Don't you worry about him." Marcy glances at Rob whose brow furrows in concentration. "Just sleep."

"But he said." I protest weakly falling into the welcoming arms of sleep.

"It's okay. We spoke to him. It's important you rest now. Do you need anything?" Rob sits on the edge of the bed and feels my forehead.

His touch comforts me. "No. I'm good. Thank you."

"You're welcome." Rob stands and nudges Marcy. They step off to the side, their voices low.

I close my eyes and welcome the respite. Drifting in and out of consciousness, I can still hear Rob and Marcy whispering.

"I'll stay." Marcy's voice raises a fraction. "You have to work in the morning. Go. I'll call if I need anything."

"Okay. I'll check in tomorrow," Rob's reply carries across my fading consciousness.

I mumble goodbye and fall into the darkness, tuning out the world at last.

When I struggle to open my eyes breaking free from a dream I can't quite remember, there's sunlight streaming through the gaps in the curtains. I stretch and slowly roll to the edge of the bed. Exhaustion slowly fades as I stand and head for the bathroom.

One glance in the mirror makes me cringe. My frizzy hair resembles an unraveling loofa. I tame it with a brush, tying it back before brushing my teeth. Considering how fucked up I was last night, I'm stunned to find I'm even able to function this morning.

Hangovers in my thirties are ten times worse than they were when I was in my twenties. Fortunately, the wine didn't linger, so there was no evidence of my blunder complete with headache and misery.

However, the memory of the night before lingers and pierces me with regret. I hide my face, embarrassed to even meet my own gaze in the mirror. How can I even show my face after that? Maybe I can gather some things and slip out the door before anyone realizes it.

Rob and Marcy were more than kind. They were amazing. I wince at the knowledge they were even present to witness the events of the night before. But in the end, I am grateful they were there in the aftermath of hurricanes Arthur and Kate.

I vaguely remember a conversation between Marcy and Rob before I drifted off. Did she stay last night? But where was Arthur?

Steeling myself for whatever I might find, I take a breath and leave the safety of the bedroom.

Marcy glances up from her seat on the couch and sets her coffee mug aside. "You're awake."

"Yeah." I shuffle closer.

"Want some coffee?" She's already on her feet and halfway to the kitchen when she asks.

"Sure." I follow and lean against the counter watching her pour the steaming brew into a plain white mug.

"Hungry? I can whip you up some eggs or pop some toast in for you if eggs are too heavy." Her concern warms my heart.

"Toast first." I smile. "Thanks, Marcy."

"Of course, what are friends for?" She puts some bread in

the toaster and gets some butter and jam out of the fridge. "Go sit at the table. I'll bring it over."

I take the chair closest to the huge window. The sun streams over the city, nearly cresting in the sky. I glance at the clock. Just after eleven am.

Marcy bustles in and sets a plate with buttered toast with a side of jam in front of me right beside my coffee. She drops into the chair next to mine and smiles.

"Feeling better today?"

"Yeah." I take a bite of the perfectly browned toast. "I'm sorry about last night."

She waves it off. "Don't even worry about it. We all have those moments, hon. I'm glad I was here to help."

The question burns my mind and I'm terrified to ask her even though I know it's inevitable. "Where's Arthur?"

"I don't know." She shrugs with a sigh. "He went out and never came back."

Fear grips me. "Aren't you worried about him?"

Marcy chuckles. "Worried? About my brother? No. I mean, I am, but not because I'm afraid something bad happened to him because he didn't come home yet. This wouldn't be the first time he wandered off to clear his head."

I sip the coffee and it warms me instantly.

"When we were kids, Arthur would wander off after an argument. Some days he wouldn't return home until after midnight." She laughed at the memory. "Mom would get so mad, but it didn't stop him."

"Where did he go?"

"No one knows. To this day, he still won't tell me where he goes to think." Marcy shakes her head. "He calls it his spot. I bet that's where he went last night. It's where he always goes, especially to get away from me."

"You're lucky." I sniff and stare out the window. "I wish I had a bond like you two have. I don't have any siblings. My dad died when I was three, and mom never remarried."

"Do you remember him?" Marcy asks, cradling her coffee mug in her hands. "Your dad."

My gaze fixes firmly on the Empire State Building. "Not really. I have a few memories, but nothing bonded us, you know?" A sad smile crosses my lips. "Mom filled in the blanks. She told me all about him." I stop myself from saying anything more knowing it will only complicate things.

"Kate." Marcy reaches across the table to take my hand. "You're not alone. I'm here for you." Her warm smile brings tears to my eyes.

"Thanks, Marcy." I wipe the tears away with my free hand. "I appreciate your support."

"Don't worry about finding a place right away either." She squeezes my hand. "If you need a place to crash, you're welcome at my place until we can find you something, okay?"

Relief washes over me. "Thank you."

"Of course." She releases me and sits back. "And we can start looking for a new job on Monday morning."

"A new job." I nod at the realization and my heart sinks. *Dad.* I won't get to see him every day. I panic.

"I mean, if you want to work for my brother, that's completely up to you."

"No. I mean, yes. You're right. I should branch out and start looking anyway. The job at the firm was only meant to be temporary anyway." I fake a smile even though my heart weeps at the thought of abandoning all contact with both my father and Arthur.

"Awesome! There might be a couple of places we can check. Oh, maybe down at the station." Marcy's already listing out possibilities, and I'm stuck, mired in my own disappointments. So much for this being an opportunity to spend time with my parents.

Marcy jumps to her feet and carries my empty plate into the kitchen. "Monday morning, for sure," she calls from the kitchen.

"What's on Monday morning?" Arthur's deep voice echoes across the room.

I gasp and spin around. He's standing beside the television wearing the same suit he wore to the office the day before. His tie is missing and a shadow darkens his jaw.

"Oh, you're alive. Good." Marcy props her hand on a hip. "I was about to call the cops and fill out a missing person's report."

"Don't you have somewhere to be?" he growls the question.

"No, actually, I don't." She glances at me. "Do you want me to help get your stuff together now?"

Arthur looks like he's been dragged down an alley and pummeled, but even worse than that, the moment she mentions gathering my stuff, Arthur's countenance darkens.

"Kate. Can we talk?" He ignores his sister's indignant huff and steps closer. His intense gaze focused solely on me. "I fucked up. I'm sorry."

My throat constricts at his apology.

"Call me if you need anything, okay, hon?" Marcy grabs her coat and escapes the apartment as though the whole building were on fire and about to explode.

Arthur's shoulders slump the moment his sister leaves. "Last night." He gestures helplessly. "I was an asshole."

"Yes, you were." I stand but don't move any closer. My hands rest on the chair maintaining a barrier between us.

"When this year started, I had plans. Big plans." He rubs his hand over his jaw. "None of these plans involved a relationship."

I bite my tongue and hold his gaze steadily. If he wants to dig himself into a deeper hole, I'll gladly let him. It'll make it easier for me to walk away.

"But that was before." He exhales, and lightning flashes in his stormy eyes. "When I found you, I never expected to feel anything this strong. It's terrifying, honestly." He scoffs. "We barely know each other, and yet I find myself wanting to not only protect you but possess you."

"Possess me?"

He licks his lower lip and nods. "All of you. Your body, your mind, all of you. I want to keep you all for myself."

"That's a bit misogynistic, Arthur." My heart races at the thought of being possessed by this man. As much as I want to deny his words affect me, I can't. Even my physical response to him leaves me confused and aroused.

"I'm not asking you to do anything against your will." He steps aside. "If you want to leave, I won't stop you. If that's what you want."

"Suddenly you care what I want?" Heat bubbles inside my chest, and I can't tell whether it's fury or passion.

"Marcy set me straight." He rests his hand on the table. "I understand why you felt you had to keep up the amnesia premise."

The amnesia...oh, God. The wine. I will never again. I pinch my eyes closed and my lapse in judgement rushes back in vivid shades of mortification. The alcohol loosened my inhibitions all right. It completely blew my cover. Shit. It was only a matter of time before the truth came out, no matter how convoluted this version is.

"I had a feeling you weren't being honest with me." Arthur watches me, his expression since. "But I misunderstood your intentions. I apologize."

I clear my throat unsure if I should rip off the bandage now and reveal the truth. But the longer the moment stretches, the more I lose my nerve.

"I apologize as well. I shouldn't have lied." The half-truth slips from my tongue in a rush. "It was selfish of me to take advantage of your kindness."

Arthur scoffs. "Kindness?" He shakes his head and laughs. "If we're being honest here, then I should confess I also had selfish reasons for my actions."

He's five feet away, but I can feel the heat pulsing between us.

"When I hit you with the door, an accident, I swear, I panicked." He swipes his hand over his face and groans. "I lied to the guards and carried you home because I was too fucking scared to call the cops and admit I injured you."

"I know." My words are soft. "I'm glad you didn't call the cops, honestly."

"It was stupid. You could have been permanently injured or died."

"You called Rob. That's almost as good as a trip to the ER

in my opinion." I chuckle. "He's a very attentive physician."

Arthur growls and his eyes darken. Possessive and jealous, he stalks closer.

I back up until the cold glass stops me. Arthur crowds me, placing his hands against the glass, caging me between his heat and the frosted pane. His eyes shift from mine, down to my mouth, and back as he studies me intently.

"That kiss haunts me, Kate." He licks his lips. "All week. I couldn't think of anything else except how much I wanted another taste."

My pulse echoes in my ears rushing like a waterfall. "Me too."

I rise up on my tip toes and end both our misery.

CHAPTER EIGHTEEN

ARTHUR

The memory of her kiss is nothing to the reality. I grip her waist, lifting her closer and angling my head. I want to devour her completely. Not a sample, not a taste. She's heady and a fizzy type of magic infuses the moment. I'm drunk on her with one kiss.

I should be terrified, but I'm not. I want more.

She arches her body against me, and I seize the invitation without hesitation. My hands slide beneath the cotton fabric. A moan breaks from deep in my throat when my fingers brush her bare skin.

There have been women over the years, but none of them seem to entice me, burrowing beneath my conscience, like Kate. I worship her curves molding them with my palms, kneading and pulling. I curse the oversized pajamas she stole from my closet.

They're my favorites. Seeing her wearing them when I walked into the apartment nearly threw my composure out the window. I've dreamed of ripping those cotton pajamas from her body every night since she arrived. It's about time I make my fantasy a reality.

Her palm slides down my chest and over my stomach. I suck in a breath when it comes to rest on my cock. Even through the fabric, the heat of her touch stokes the fire hotter.

As much as I want to strip her down and take her up against the glass in view of the whole city, I refrain. We have all the time in the world to christen each surface of my apartment. Right now, I need her sprawled beneath me while I memorize her glorious, bare skin with my mouth.

Without warning, I scoop her into my arms. She squeals and clings to me.

"What are you doing?" She laughs as I carry her into the

bedroom.

"I intended to take you up against those windows at some point." I whisper against her temple. "But right now, I have other plans for you."

I set her down on the bed and step back enough to give me room to strip. I toss my coat off to the side. Kate lays back against the pillows and watches me. Her parted lips and glassy eyes betray her hunger.

Instead of rushing to strip, I slowly unbutton my shirt while holding her lust filled gaze. She runs her fingertip down the vee of her top and mimics my motions. Every button I release, she matches. The creamy expanse of skin she reveals leaves me speechless. Her soft, ample curves push against the fabric, and her deep breaths reveal more. She arches her brow when I pull the shirt off my shoulders and toss it aside.

Kate shakes her head. The blue fabric barely covers her areolas. I need to see her breasts in their full glory, but she gestures to my waist.

"Pants next." Her husky voice makes my cock painfully hard.

I unfasten my belt and slide the button free. As I push the pants down over my hips, Kate again surprises me. Her hand slides beneath the waistband of her bottoms. The moment her fingertips reach her cleft, her eyes drift closed and her breath hitches.

"Tease." I kick my pants and underwear aside before climbing into the bed.

She opens her eyes and moans softly. Her cheeks are flushed. I watch the fabric gently moving in rhythmic motions.

I grasp the fabric and pull it down her legs. She lifts her ass enough to allow them to slide free.

"Fuck, Kate." My gaze fixes on her delicate hand with two fingers pressed against her clit.

I press soft kisses along the inside of her thighs as I nudge them open, revealing her pussy slick with her arousal. I remove her hand and replace her fingers with my tongue.

Kate's moan echoes off the bedroom walls. Encouraged by

the sound, I flick my tongue deeper between her folds, boldly tasting her. She's sweet and addicting. I suck her clit into my mouth and she arches off the bed.

God, she's responsive. I grip her hips with my hands, and she buries her fingers in my hair. Every tug only emboldens me. I spread her wider and give myself better access. She's mine, all mine, and I intend to savor each drop her when she comes against my mouth.

My name sounds sinful intertwined with her whimpered moans. Her breath quickens and I hear it catch as I push her higher and higher. When I slip two fingers into her, she bucks against my mouth. I find a generous rhythm between my mouth and my hand.

The telltale flutter against my fingertips warns me she's close. I redouble my efforts wanting her to surrender to me with her climax.

"Fuck. Oh, fuck." She mutters over and over when she comes. Her body clenches around my fingers. I smile as she slowly comes down from her blissful high. But I don't relent completely until she's trembling, her hands flexing against my scalp trying to push me away.

I pull back enough to study her face and wipe my mouth with the back of my hand. Better than a five-star meal, hands down.

A lopsided blissful smile pulls at her mouth. "That was amazing."

"You think that was amazing?" I scoff, climbing up over her until our noses touch. "That was just the appetizer."

She kisses me, and I melt against her. This time I take her full breast in my hand and roll her nipple between my fingertips. She gasps into the kiss and presses her body closer.

I trail kisses down over her jaw and capture a ripe nipple in my mouth sucking it until it pebbles against my tongue. Kate's urgent moans only intensify my need to pace myself. I want her so desperate for me she'll come even harder.

Kate scratches her fingernails over my head, her moans reverberate through my body. I dedicate attention to both breasts until she's writhing against me.

"Please, Arthur. Please." She licks her lips and gasps when I flick my tongue over her nipple.

"What do you need, sweetheart?" I lean back.

She arches her hips against my thigh. "I need you."

"Say the words," I whisper against her mouth before kissing her gently.

"Fuck me."

I chuckle at the crass demand. "Wouldn't you rather I make love to you?"

"Make love to me, fuck me, I don't care. All I want is you inside me...now." She wraps her legs around mine.

"Let me get protection." I murmur, leaning over to the nightstand drawer.

"Shit." She mutters under her breath and sighs. Her smile fades a fraction until I slide the condom down over my cock.

"Is this what you wanted?" I pull her close and slide the tip over her sensitive cleft.

Her gasp ends on a moan. "Yes." She clings tightly to me, her fingernails biting into my shoulders, when I push inside.

Kate tosses her head back. I sink deeper until I'm seated fully inside her. Fuck, she fits like a favorite pair of gloves. Her body grips me tight.

"How does that feel?" I nip the tender spot on her throat right below her ear. She shivers and holds tight.

"So good." She bites her lower lip and meets my gaze.

I kiss her and move, starting slowly and gently increasing momentum. She's tight and warm. It's been so long since I've been with anyone, I'm worried I may come too quickly.

Kate meets my thrusts with her own. I let her take control of the pace. She urges me faster. I close my eyes trying to keep from ending this before it's even had a chance to start.

She gently presses her hand to my heart. "Lie down."

"Something wrong?" I move to pull out, but she stops me.

With a little effort, she rolls me onto my back without unsheathing me from her warmth. Staring up at her, I'm struck dumb. She's fucking stunning as she shucks the top and shakes her hair back.

Her bewitching gaze locks on mine and she grinds her hips down taking me deeper than before.

"Holy shit." I rest my hands on her hips and inhale deep. "You're gonna make me lose control if you do that, sweetheart."

"Mmmm, I like the thought of you losing control." She leans forward, her hair creating a curtain of dark waves around her flushed face. "I won't break. I like it rough."

The thought alone gives my cock a burst of strength. "Show me, baby." I lick my dry lips. "Take what you want."

She pouts. I wrap my hand around her delicate throat and kiss her mouth firmly. "I'll give you what you need later."

Her eyes glitter with lust and her hips buck against mine. She thrusts at her own pace, slowly increasing the tempo, using me until she's panting.

"That's it, sweetheart. Come for me." The words trigger something inside her.

Kate's mouth opens on a breathless scream, and I hold my fingertips against her pulse. She rubs her clit against me enough to trigger her climax. I drop my hands to her hips and thrust up, pounding into her until my own release rushes up and capsizes us both in a listless ocean of sexual satisfaction.

Weak from the intensity of her orgasm, she collapses against my chest. I wrap my arms around her and hold her close. Slowly, our overheated bodies cool and our breathing slows. I run my fingers along her spine, stroking her like a contented kitten curled in my lap.

I've never had sex rock me to my core. Even with the most enthusiastic lovers, sex was passable at best. Normally I'd find any excuse to leave, but now I'm desperate for any reason to stay, to keep her like this forever. But, holy hell, this is unlike anything I've ever experienced.

My heartbeat mimics hers. How is it possible to be so synchronized with someone at such a basic level and yet be practical strangers? One thing is certain, I want to know everything about her. What she likes. Her favorite things. What makes her smile.

Fate may have blindsided me when she appeared in my life. I was a fool to fight it, but now I have no intention of letting her go.

I slowly roll her onto the bed and kiss her forehead before pulling the blanket over her.

She sighs sleepily and smiles. "Where are you going?"

"To clean up." I kiss her head again. "Rest now. I have plans for you."

"Promises, promises." Kate snuggles deeper into the blankets.

Halfway to the bathroom, I glance over my shoulder at the woman in my bed.

Kate looks so vulnerable and sated. A warmth infuses me and wraps its tendrils around my heart. I didn't expect to find someone who would make me feel this much contentment.

In the bathroom, I toss the condom into the trash and turn on the shower. The heat renews my energy. Under the spray, I wash away the uncertainty and regrets. This is a new day, a new opportunity. I wash the sweat from my skin, but the memories remain. When I close my eyes to rinse off the soap, a sweet floral scent surrounds me.

The press of her body against mine has my cock jumping in response.

"I thought you were resting?"

"While you're in here all naked and wet?" She slides her slick body against mine and wraps her hand around my cock.

"Damn it, Kate." Her hand gives enough pressure to make me see stars. I brace my weight against the wall and the water sluices over us both. I swear again when she strokes twice and drops to her knees.

My Kate. Mine. It doesn't matter where she came from or what troubles lay in her past, together we can face anything.

When her mouth closes around my cock, I lose all coherent thought and surrender to this wonderfully wicked woman.

CHAPTER NINETEEN
KATHERINE

Hot water runs over me as I take him in my mouth. I'm not a fan of oral. Maybe it's because I never had a partner I trusted to give me what I needed or trusted my own abilities to reciprocate.

Arthur makes me feel like a goddess. He worships my body. My insecurities faded the moment he kissed me, and then disappeared when I saw the look of hunger on his face in the bedroom. Emboldened, I teased him, pushing him to the bounds of his restraint. I fucking loved every moment.

He let me take control. This is the first time I was able to tell a partner what I needed. While Arthur knows what he wants and how he wants it, he gave me the reins and let me take control. When he disappeared into the bathroom and I heard the shower running, it drew me like a siren's call.

I wanted him, even after he made me come. Twice. I've never even been able to bring myself relief like he did. He knew exactly what my body needed.

My tongue strokes the length of his cock and it pulses against my lips. I know exactly what he needs, and I'm more than happy to give it to him. His balls rest in my right hand while the left encircles his shaft teasing the head of his cock.

"Kate." He groans and his legs tremble. "Deeper, sweetheart." He gasps when I slide him in as far as I can. "Good girl."

His praise emboldens me. I quicken my pace alternating pressure with my hand and my mouth. His hips rock back and forth almost until he's fucking my mouth gently. I intensify my efforts and am rewarded with a whimper.

Water runs over my face. I close my eyes and focus only on pleasing him. After his magnificent tongue brought me a toe-curling orgasm, I want to give him a gift of my own.

"Damn, sweetheart, I'm going to come. If you..."

I quicken my pace determined to swallow every last drop. He tries to pull away, but I grip him tighter.

Arthur's groan echoes off the tiles mingling with the steam from the shower. His cum coats my tongue. I swallow quickly, gently working the length of him to wring his body into submission. He trembles beneath my touch.

Pride suffuses me. I rise to my feet and he pulls me under the spray holding me against him, his face buried against my throat. He rocks me gently until he regains his senses.

"That was amazing." He kisses me deeply. "You're amazing."

There's no shame, no disappointment, no judgement between us. Nothing but pure satisfaction.

He shakes free from his thoughts and smiles. "I'll let you rinse off."

"Okay."

When he steps from the shower, uncertainty consumes me. I like having him near me, but I know there are still things unspoken between us we need to address if we're going to make this relationship work. Like the truth of where I come from.

He wraps a towel around himself and leaves me alone in the bathroom. I take the moment of peace to wash quickly and put some conditioner in my hair to keep it from looking like a poufy disaster. Once I reach a semblance of cleanliness, I dry off and wrap the towel around my body and another around my hair.

Arthur isn't in the bedroom. I hear noise in the living room, so I peek out the door. He's in the kitchen sorting through the cabinets.

"Looking for something?" I walk in the room blotting my hair dry.

"Food." The towel hangs low on his hips. One tug and I could have it around his feet.

"There's some leftovers from the other night in the fridge." I walk past him, trailing my fingertips over his lower back. I bend at the waist when I reach into the fridge to pull out the containers.

"We could order take out." His voice echoes behind me.

I freeze when his hand slides beneath my towel and glides over my sex. My legs part of their own volition.

"But that would mean I have to get dressed." I glance at him over my shoulder.

"This is true." His grin transforms his face with a mischievous charm. "I much prefer you naked."

"You can't be ready for me again?" I arch my brow and moan when he slides one finger into me.

"Are you complaining?" he asks with a smirk. "Damn it, you're so wet. Maybe I should have another taste. A little dessert before dinner."

I straighten quickly knowing my legs won't hold me if he continues to tease me. His hand falls to his side.

"Let's eat first." I set to arranging some leftovers on plates and putting them in the microwave.

Arthur wraps his arms around my waist and pulls me firmly against him. The towel slips and he captures my breasts in his hands. His merciless lips tease along my throat.

I brace myself. He's relentless and commanding. I love every minute, every touch.

The microwave timer goes off.

"Arthur."

"Hmmm." He moans against my throat.

"Your food is ready." I try to pull it from the microwave, but he's distracting me. I nearly drop it.

"After food. After!" Trying to pry myself from his grasp is nearly impossible. But I'm able to shake him off long enough to put the plate in his hand. "Go. Eat."

"Yes, ma'am." His teasing smile flashes, and I swear my body went *sploosh*. If he keeps this up, I'm going to run out of dry underwear quickly.

Once my food is heated through, I join him at the table.

We eat quickly and in silence. I hadn't realized how hungry I was. After last night, I wasn't sure if I would be hungry at all today, let alone be in the mood for sex.

Arthur's gaze drifts from the skyline to me. The sun is starting to descend over the city. The Empire State Building casts a long shadow over the buildings near it.

I collect both of our empty plates and put them in the sink. When I come back, Arthur's sitting in front of the oversized window.

"Come here." He pulls me down into his lap.

Joy overwhelms me. His arms lock around my waist and I nestle my head against his shoulder. Together we stare out over the Manhattan.

"I love this view of the city." He lets his hand run across my thigh, slipping beneath the cotton towel as he travels the path up to my hip.

"It's perfect." My gaze lingers on the Empire State Building, then on the twin towers beyond it. I turn and study Arthur's profile, ignoring the tug of guilt deep in the pit of my soul.

"Millions of people down there." He teases the seam where my thighs meet and parts them with a gentle nudge. "All blissfully ignorant of everything around them."

A moan catches in my throat at the gentle pressure of his fingertip on my clit. I'm embarrassingly wet from his teasing earlier. He coats his fingers in it before making slow circles over the sensitive bud.

I cling tighter to him. "Arthur." His name is a plea, an offering, an admonishment all wrapped together in delicious heat.

He continues to tease me, taking his sweet time, bringing me close and then easing the pressure. Within moments he has me panting, trembling against him, I can't stop myself from begging.

"Please, Arthur. Please. I need to come."

In an instant, he drops his hand and lifts me to my feet. I stumble forward and catch myself against the window. My towel falls away. I'm completely bare in front of the whole city of New York, if they cared to look up. The thought sends a bolt of need straight to my pussy.

Arthur's heat presses into me. His towel is gone. I know

because his cock brushes against my ass when I lean into him. He pins my wrists against the glass and nudges my stance wider with his foot.

"Keep your hands on the glass, Kate," he whispers against my ear. "No matter what. I want you to keep your hands right there. Do you understand?"

I exhale and fog the glass with my breath. "Yes."

"Good girl." He slides his hands down my arms, over my torso, until they rest on my hips. He pulls my ass against him.

I'm shaking. The cold glass does little to chill the flame burning through me. I tilt my hips giving him access to the place I want him most.

His hand smooths over my hip before disappearing. I open my mouth to protest in disappointment, but the loud crack followed by the sting of his hand connecting with my ass brings me up short.

"What the hell?" I glare at him and my hand slips from the position against the window.

He brings his hand down on the opposite cheek and I quickly reposition it. Pain and pleasure radiate through me.

"I told you not to move." He wraps his hand around my throat and strokes with a hint of pressure.

"Why did you spank me?" My outrage dims at the caress. It's difficult to remain outraged when it's what I crave.

"Did you lie to me?" He takes the lobe of my ear between his teeth and tugs.

"No." I whimper.

"You told me you like it rough." He presses his cock against the cleft of my ass.

I thrust my hips back against him. "Yes, please."

With his hand on my throat, he positions his cock at my entrance and slides in with little effort. I'm soaking wet, practically weeping for him to fill me.

"You feel so good, Kate." He nips at my earlobe again and his grip on my throat tightens a fraction.

There's no way to stifle the moans as he thrusts into me. He has me pinned where he wants me, taking me without mercy, without hesitation. I focus on maintaining my position against the glass and see his reflection. The focused concentration and firm set of his lips as he drives deeper into me. Fuck, yes. This is what I've been missing.

As if reading my body, Arthur shifts his grip on my throat to my breasts, rolling each nipple in turn sending shockwaves of pleasure ricocheting through my limbs. I'm helpless, and yet I know he's there ready to catch me should my legs fail. He caught me at my weakest moment, even though it went against his judgement. He caught me. My knight. Arthur.

A spiral of pressure unfurls in the pit of my stomach. I'm going to come; all I need is a gentle push over the edge.

"Please, I'm...please." My words are broken, but Arthur knows.

"That's it, baby, come for me." He reaches between my folds and applies the perfect amount of pressure to send me cascading over the waterfall. I tumble headfirst into my orgasm, my fingers trying to dig into the unforgiving glass.

He thrusts a few more times before pulling out. I feel the hot spray of his release against my back, and I smile at his consideration. Although the thought of him coming inside me makes my pussy clench with another spasm.

"Don't move." He disappears, and I take the moment of reprieve to catch my breath.

Arthur returns and wipes me clean with a damp rag. "Did I hurt you?"

I turn and wrap my weakened arms around him. He holds me steady and kisses me. I'll never get enough of this man. He holds me and we linger, mouths searching, our actions speaking louder than words ever could.

The kiss breaks and we're both breathless. He rests his head against mine.

"Thank you." Satisfaction seeps into my bones.

He grins. "You're welcome."

Together we stand naked in the window staring out over the city. The prominent buildings stand tall against the failing light and reality slowly consumes me. The towers. The Empire State

Building. Mom. Dad.

I press my eyes closed and a tear slips free even in the midst of the most amazing sexual encounter of my life, I'm caught up in a life not my own. And for the first time, I'm terrified of losing what I found here. Of losing Arthur.

"Are you crying?" He tips my chin to glance at my face.

I swipe my tears away and sniff.

"What's wrong?" His tone is gentle, and I know I have to tell him the truth even though it's unfathomable.

Mustering all the courage I have, I take a breath and face him. "There's something you should know."

He leans forward to kiss me, and I stop him, my hand against his chest. Concern fills his steel blue gaze.

"My name is Katherine Cohen." I brace myself and push through. "And I'm from the future."

Whatever expression I expected, Arthur exceeds it with spectacular flourish. Disbelief makes him laugh, but when I don't join in, he sobers instantly.

I know whatever we shared has fractured, and I wish I could take it back the moment he releases me and puts space between us. The last year of my life might have been horrible, but it's nothing compared to the pain of the man I love staring at me the way he is now.

CHAPTER TWENTY
ARTHUR

Part of me thinks this is a joke, but her expression is fragile and earnest. I shake my head and step back, running my hand through my hair. She reaches for me, but I need answers first. Her touch will only cloud me with confusion.

I need to think, damn it, but it's difficult when her scent still clings to me and the evidence of our lovemaking surrounds us. I snatch the towel off the floor and wrap it around my waist.

Kate does the same, wrapping the fabric tightly around her torso. I'm almost saddened at the loss but right now I need to focus. Both of us being naked doesn't help at all.

Her eyes fill with tears and she bites her lower lip. She's searching for something to say, I can almost see the gears spinning in her mind.

She can't be serious, can she? Cohen? As in Victor Cohen, my colleague? None of this makes any sense. After spending my whole life in this city, I've heard some crazy stories, but this one definitely takes the grand prize. I can't help but feel like she's toying with me, but she's upset and I can tell it's sincere. I groan and try to face this information with an analytical mind.

"Katherine Cohen." When I speak her name, she snaps to attention. "That's your full birth name."

She nods and a sad smile parts her lips. "Mom didn't want me to have a middle name."

"And your date of birth?" I monitor her reaction to each question carefully.

"June 24, 1985." She cringes.

"I see." But I really don't. If she's telling me the truth, then she hasn't even been born yet. "And you're from the city?"

"Yes. We lived in Manhattan until..." She pauses and drops her gaze. "When I turned four, we moved to Staten Island to live with my grandma."

"Why?" I press.

Tears fall fresh pooling in the corners of her eyes and spilling down her cheeks. "Dad died."

An icy tendril of dread touched the base of my neck. "Kate, who is your father?"

She hiccups and her voice cracks. "Victor Cohen."

The events of the past two weeks fall into place, and I stumble back until my knees buckle and I collapse against the couch arm. "Is this why you were outside my office on New Year's Day? You were looking for him?"

She hides her tearstained red face behind her hands. "Yes."

I shake my head in disbelief. The questions she asked about him, every conversation they shared. Her smiles. Her laughter. She wasn't in love with him in the way I assumed. Not even close. But none of this explains how the hell any of this is possible.

"This can't be possible." The gruff edge to my voice makes her jump. "How the hell did you end up here?"

"I don't know." She uses the edge of the towel to wipe her face and sniffs trying to contain her emotions. "One minute I'm standing on the observation deck, and the next I'm seeing the sun rise with the twin towers."

Her words are pure nonsense. "What do you mean?"

Kate stomps her feet and groans. "I can't tell you what it means even if I wanted to. That's like the first rule of time travel. No spoilers! I don't want to be the reason we declare war with Canada and dinosaurs rule the future."

More gibberish pours from her mouth. "Wait? What the hell are you talking about now?"

She sighs heavily and collapses in one of the dining room chairs. The towel rides up her thigh. I refocus my attention on her face wishing I had told her to put some damn clothes on before we dove into the specifics.

"Haven't you seen *Back to the Future*...shit, never mind." She pinches the bridge of her nose. "I can't tell you what's going to happen in the future because it could alter future events causing a rip in the space-time continuum. Or a paradox. Or an alternate timeline. I mean, there are a lot of theories as to what would really happen, but I am *not* interested in finding out which one got it right."

I fold my arms across my chest. "Well, it may be a bit late for that considering you've told me you're from the future and your dad dies when you're four." I push aside the anguish attached to this knowing I'll have to address this piece of information later, but she's right, we can't take the chance of altering the future for personal gain.

"Shit." She bites her thumbnail. "But if we don't interfere in any events, then nothing will change, right?"

I laugh. "Kate. The door must have hit you harder than I thought." The possibilities are too fantastical for me to believe a word out of her mouth.

"You don't believe me?" The color drains from her face.

"You want me to believe you're the daughter of my colleague who's come from the future." I do the math in my head. "From what year?" I lean forward.

"2020."

"Ah," I reply as though it's obvious. "You don't know how you got here or why."

"No idea."

I nod and slowly rise to my feet. "Maybe I should call Rob and have him see if they can get you in for a scan down at the hospital?"

Kate jumps to her feet and charges toward me. "There's nothing wrong with my head!"

Those delectable lips and delicious curves I enjoyed only an hour ago distract me from the truth. The girl is delusional. She has to be. None of this makes any sense.

"Sweetheart," I place my hands on her shoulders ignoring my body's response to the smooth texture of her skin and the heat simmering between us. "There's nothing to worry about. I'll call Rob, and we'll get this figured out."

"You think I'm crazy." She wrenches herself away. "I'm not crazy."

"I never said you were crazy." I reach for her but she's already sprinting toward the bedroom.

I'm on her heels, but she slams the door in my face. "Kate. Kate!"

Silence reaches me. "Shit."

I cross the room and pick up the phone. Rob doesn't answer at his place, so I call the hospital. When the nurse tells me he's with a patient, I leave my name and ask for her to have him call me right away.

The bedroom door opens, and Kate emerges wearing the same clothes I found her in on New Year's Day. She crosses to the door and gets her oversized wool coat.

"Where are you going?" I stand between her and the door blocking her exit. "I can't let you leave. You need help."

A glare, one I can only describe as murderous, pins me in place. She hisses in a breath. "You have no right to keep me captive here. I'm perfectly sound in body and mind. Now move, before I move you."

A good six inches shorter than me, Kate poses no threat. I scoff and hold my ground.

"It's not safe for you out there. I've called Rob. He'll help, just stay here, Kate. We'll figure this all out." My pleas fall on stubborn ears.

"There's nothing for me to figure out." She jabs her finger in my chest. "You, on the other hand." Her shoulders shrug with the implication of her words. Determination flashes in her mismatched eyes.

I lift my hands in supplication. "Explain it to me then, Kate."

She shakes her head and the determination in her gaze fades into sadness. "I tried, Arthur. I bared my soul with the truth."

"The truth?" I scoff, but sober the moment she scowls. "I'm a practical man, but I'm sorry, your truth goes against all reason."

"Goodbye, Arthur." She tries to push past me and grab the door handle, but I block her. "Move."

"No. You're not going anywhere." I wrap my hand around

her wrist and tug her away from the door, but she bristles at the touch.

"Let me go." The low growl of her voice sets off warning bells in my head.

"Not until we get to the bottom of this." My grip tightens, and I pull her against me.

Without hesitation, she jabs her elbow into my side with her weight, stomps on my foot, slams the back of her fist into my nose, and drives her elbow into my groin.

Pain radiates through me. I double over in agony and stumble forward, blood dripping from my nose onto the carpet.

By the time I regain some of my senses, I realize Kate's gone. Gingerly, I hobble into the bedroom, glaring at the phone on the other side of the apartment. I should call the guard on the ground floor, but what would that accomplish? If she's willing to injure me to this degree for her freedom, then I have to let her go.

Warmth coats my face. Shit. I'm bleeding everywhere. I stumble into the bathroom and run the water, washing my face in the sink and blotting the mess smeared across me with white towels. Fuck, my bathroom is a murder scene.

The ache in my side and foot dissipates long before the throbbing where her elbow connected with my balls. It takes much longer to stem the waterfall of blood coming from my nose. It's already turning purple. Great. I gently press the side of my nose, and there's a screaming pain. Yup, it's broken.

Looks like I'll be paying Rob a visit at the ER. As I pull on some old clothes, I worry about Kate. Obviously, she's lost, but what if she's telling the truth?

This is crazy. Time travel isn't real. There's no way in hell. It's science fiction, not reality.

But the more I think about it, I can't shake the feeling there's a piece of this puzzle missing. Maybe I should give her time and space. Kate may not be dangerous to anyone but herself at this point. Except my well-ordered life.

First, I need to deal with the broken nose she left me along with a broken heart.

CHAPTER TWENTY-ONE
KATHERINE

Guilt and anger twist in the pit of my stomach gnawing away at my insides leaving a dark void of regret. Maybe I shouldn't have told him. It's a lot of information, and even though it conflicts with his perception of reality, it doesn't negate the truth.

I don't belong here. And by extension, I don't belong with him.

Assaulting him when he blocked the door may have been a stretch, but I knew he would never let me go of his own volition. Not since he truly thinks I'm a mental case. No, I had to get out of there before he locked me up in the psych ward. Mimicking Gracie Lou Freebush and her dramatic display of self-defense, I gave myself the window I needed. Oh God, I probably broke his nose. He'll definitely be sporting a pair of black eyes and some bruises in the morning.

If Arthur thought I was crazy before, he certainly will now.

When I reach the ground floor, I half expect the doorman to stop me or have security throw up barricades hindering my escape. But I walk out the doors without any issue. The attendant even holds the door open and wishes me a good evening.

The cold evening air stings my cheeks. I walk along the street tugging the wool collar higher to block the wind from my face.

My act of instinctive defiance ensures several things. I have no job, no home, and no belongings. I did manage to grab the cash he gave me for my first payday. But a hundred bucks isn't going to get me far.

I find the first subway station and stare at the signs. I should try to find a shelter for the night, at least then I won't be sleeping under the bridge down by the river. But instead, I take the line to the Upper West Side.

The address is a fixed point in my memory. I don't remember the details, but Mom told me stories about their first place on 73rd.

After a quick ride, I emerge from underground and integrate myself into the bustling Saturday night pedestrian traffic. Normally I enjoyed the anonymity of walking the city without anyone noticing my presence, but tonight it leaves me anxious and lonely.

My feet take me down the sidewalks and around the corners past shops and restaurants. I admire the hustle of the city. Some of these things will still be here years from now. Some won't, and that's the part twisting a hole in my sanity.

Obviously, there's no way for me to get back to 2020. I don't have much keeping me there, but here in 1985, I'm an outsider with too much knowledge. It would be simple to use it to my advantage and manipulate the future ensuring my success.

I'm no expert on quantum mechanics and the physics of space and time, but I know doing so would be playing with fire. Fear seizes me. What if I've already ruined something by telling Arthur? Does it matter? He doesn't believe me anyway.

I thought he did. Then I saw the cognitive dissidence jerk him right back into denial. Tears appear again, and I blink them away. No. No more tears. I can't change him. I can't make him understand. I can't control anything but my own actions and how I respond.

In one of the last conversations I had with Mom, she imparted these words of wisdom. She admitted it took her years to realize their truth, but when she applied it to her life, it made things more manageable.

I'd lost my job. My apartment. Justin and I were on the rocks, and with her in hospice, I knew it was only a matter of time before I lost her too. I didn't want useless platitudes and deep insights on life. I wanted something I could grasp with both hands and hold tight. I was losing control and it scared the fucking shit out of me.

Her words echo in my mind giving me strength with each

step.

When I reach number twenty-three, I stop and stare up at the narrow brick townhouse squeezed between neighboring buildings. Light illuminates the first-floor window. They're home.

Mom and Dad. Alive. Happy. Excited for their future family, with me. My grin falters. No, not *me*. I pause on the bottom step.

What the hell am I doing here? I should leave before they see me. They don't need my drama. It was stupid of me to think I could scavenge whatever time I could with them stuck in this nightmare time slip.

"Kate?"

A dictionary of curse words zings through my brain at lightning speed. I regain my composure and spin around. Dad's standing on the sidewalk with a bag of groceries in one arm. His warm smile and kind eyes instantly soothe the ache in my heart.

"Hi, Da...Victor." I wave and sway catching myself against the railing.

"Whoa, easy there. These steps can get slippery sometimes."

"Yeah. I'm good."

"Did Arthur send you?" He chuckles. "I swear sometimes he can't turn off work. The man needs a hobby or a wife."

My throat constricts at the mention of his name. "No."

Dad's smile falters. "Is something wrong? Did something happen?"

I shake my head, but there's no stopping the tears. My lip trembles and I fight hard to keep myself from falling apart on my parent's front steps.

"Kate?" Mom's voice echoes behind me.

I tumble over the precipice and burst into tears.

"Oh, honey." Mom rushes down the steps, careful not to slip, and wraps her arms around me. "Victor, what happened?"

"I don't know. One minute we're talking, and the next—"

"Come on, honey. Let's go inside. You need a cup of tea and something to eat." She tucks my hair behind my ears. "Then you can tell me what's wrong."

I can't fight her kindness or her tender touch. I missed it so much. All I can do is nod and follow her up the stairs.

Inside, she tugs off my coat and deposits me on the couch. "You sit here, and I'll be right back. I have a kettle already on the stove."

"Thank you, M...Nora."

"Of course." Mom carries my coat into the hallway. I can hear their voices carry down the hall, but I can't make out the words.

My gaze drifts over the room. The avocado green and goldenrod patterned sofas seem to be holdovers from the seventies, but the rest of the room is tame enough. The pictures on the wall opposite the front window catch my attention.

I cross the room and inspect them. Mom and Dad at their wedding. Grandma and Grandpa on their front porch. A few other familiar family members are scattered across the wall, but I keep coming back to their wedding photo.

"We got married in Las Vegas." Mom comes up beside me with two mugs in her hands. "I told him I wanted a house, not a wedding. So we compromised."

I take the mug she offers and blow across the top. "You look so happy."

"It wasn't traditional, but it was fun." She laughs. "I even allowed Elvis to officiate the ceremony."

"I remember." The gaffe slips from my tongue and I sputter in an attempt to correct myself. "Arthur mentioned it."

Her brow rises. "I'm surprised Arthur pays attention to anything aside from his business." She waves her hand. "He's a wonderful man and a good friend of ours, but the man does nothing but work."

"I noticed."

Mom gestures to the couch, and I sit down beside her. We both take a sip of tea and it warms me instantly.

"Feeling better?" she asks.

"Yes, thank you." I clear my throat and shift uncomfortably. "I apologize for breaking down like that. It's been—" I heave a shaky exhale. "—A rough couple of months."

"Do you want to talk about it?" Her understanding smile nearly breaks my heart. She's so damn young, but I see her older self beneath the surface. It takes all my restraint to keep the tears from bursting over the dam again.

"I shouldn't." I shake my head. "It's complicated, and I don't want to drag you into my drama."

"Honey, don't you worry about dragging me anywhere. You seem like you need a friend, and I'm glad you had the sense to come here." She pats my hand. "Now, what did he do?"

I laugh. I can't help it. Mom always was too observant for her own good.

"Are you talking about Arthur?" Dad comes in and sits in the armchair a few feet away.

My face warms. I don't want to talk about what happened with Arthur in front of my parents, but they don't know how awkward this whole situation is. How could they? I take a fortifying sip of tea and cradle it in my hands.

"Honey, we already know there's something between you two." Mom nudges me. "Victor told me about it on Monday night. Why do you think I came to the office this week?" She winks. "I had to meet the woman who caught Arthur's attention."

I nearly choke. "But...we weren't even talking then."

Dad snorts. "Yeah, Arthur was in a right foul mood all week." He laughs. "I even caught him working on the wrong proposal."

"See?" Mom lifts her mug in salute. "You've got him all kinds of distracted. Besides, I saw the chemistry between you two. Positively nuclear."

This conversation has taken a strange turn, but I forge ahead thankful to even have the two most important people in my life in the same room with me.

With a deep breath, I launch into a brief, non-descriptive account of my relationship with Arthur touching lightly on the events of the last twenty-four hours leading up to this moment.

Their reactions range from horrified to angry to appeased and then circle right back again. Only I don't reveal exactly what caused the fight, but the mere mention of an argument has Dad on his feet.

"Why is he so stubborn?" He stalks toward the door. "I'm going to march over there and give him a piece of my mind."

"Sit down, Victor," Mom admonishes him. "You're not going anywhere. This is between Kate and Arthur." She turns back to me. "I'm sure he'll come to his senses at some point during the night."

Thoughts of Arthur and his sore...ego and busted nose make me cringe. "I doubt it."

Mom tilts her head in concern. "Do you need a place to stay?"

"No. Thank you. I couldn't impose."

"It's not imposition. We have a spare room for guests, and it'd be nice to get a chance to get to know you better."

My soul warms at her words. "I'd love that."

"Good, it's settled. I'll get the spare room ready after dinner." Mom gestures to the kitchen. "I need to check on the roast."

After Mom leaves, I catch Dad staring at me when I reach for my tea. "Something wrong?"

He shakes his head. "No. It's just...I have this odd feeling about you. Who are your parents?"

I nearly spit out the tea and sputter before swallowing it. "Uh. Why do you say that?"

Dad leans close. "Your eyes. Two different colors, like mine." He chuckles. "It's not a common trait. We could be related. How crazy would that be?"

"Crazy." I reply uncertain of what I should say.

"Don't worry about Arthur." He winks. "He'll come around."

"I hope you're right." I finish my tea and stand. "Where's the kitchen? I'll take my cup in."

"Don't worry about it. You're our guest." Dad takes my cup and gathers up the others. "Relax."

Once he leaves, I stand and pace the floor. This feels so surreal, staying with my parents like this. I wander down the hall and peer into the rooms taking an inventory of the home's layout.

The phone rings and I nearly jump out of my skin.

"Hello." Dad's voice echoes from the kitchen.

I lean against the wall and listen.

"Yes, she's here." He pauses. "No. She's staying here." Another pause. "Okay. I'll let her know. Bye."

"Who was it?" Mom asks him.

"Arthur's sister, Marcy. She was looking for Kate."

Fear grips me. He knows I'm here. I can't stay. Not now. Without waiting for Mom and Dad to come find me, I bolt down the hallway, grab my coat, and venture back out into the cold.

I don't know where I'll end up, but I let my feet carry me wherever my heart leads.

Chapter Twenty-Two
Arthur

The cold, sterile hospital environment does nothing to settle my anxiety. Where the hell did she go? I made sure to call Marcy before I left my place, in case Kate tried to contact her. Did she even have my sister's number? Or her address?

I press the towel covered bag of peas against my nose. They're turning to mush in the bag, but they're still cold and soothing. While it treats my physical discomfort, it does nothing to soothe the gaping hole in my conscience.

The more I think about Kate's confession, the more I realize how horribly I reacted. I should have been more understanding. She's obviously in some kind of delusional state caused by her injury. Now she's out roaming the city with nowhere to go.

A gentle knock on the door stirs me from my thoughts. Rob enters the room with a clipboard in his hand. He glances up and freezes instantly.

"What the hell happened to you?" He closes the door and sets the board aside.

"I ran into a door." My pride hurts enough, I can't bring myself to tell Rob the truth.

He pulls on a pair of clean gloves and nudges the cold bag from my face. His eyes narrow as he inspects the damage. I wince as he presses and prods my face, asking stupid questions about whether this hurts and then jamming his thumb into the aching protrusion that used to be my nose.

I hiss and mumble one-word responses littered with a few choice swear words to emphasize my enthusiasm.

"It's broken. I'll have to reset it."

"Do whatever you need to do." I brace myself

He braces his hands on my face and screaming pain

ricochets through me as he applies pressure. There's a distinct crack as it realigns.

"Son of a bitch!" My whole body trembles at the rush of pain and immediate release of pressure. The ache remains, but it doesn't throb like it did before.

Rob backs away and prepares some bandages. "So, you going to tell me who hit you?"

I scoff. Rob's too observant. This makes him an amazing physician, but it also makes him an annoying friend. I've never been able to hide anything from him.

"Kate." I dab the towel to my nose to catch any remaining blood.

"Kate did this to you?" Rob's laughter fills the small room. When he sees my serious expression, he sobers. "Wait, you're serious?"

"Have you ever known me to joke about anything like this in my life?"

"Good point." Rob grabs a few pills from a bottle and pours me a small cup of water. "Take these. They'll help with swelling and pain."

I pop them in my mouth and wash them down.

Rob leans against the counter and crosses his arms. "What the hell happened?"

Deflated, I shake my head. "I don't know. One minute we're all over each other and then the next she's spinning some crazy story."

"Hold up," Rob interjects. "You two had sex?"

I nod. "Yeah, I came home this morning and well, we worked things out."

"I'm glad you came to your senses." He eyes me with skepticism. "After your behavior last night, you're lucky I didn't break your nose first."

"I admit. I was an asshole." I replace the ice pack on the right side of my nose. "I came home this morning and apologized. Then things got a little heated."

"You two fucked like rabbits." Rob nods. "I get the point, please feel free to skip to the part where she kicks your ass."

"After the most amazing sex I've ever had…" I pause for emphasis and to annoy Rob, stopping only to admire the look of disgust on his face. "She tells me the truth."

"She never lost her memory?" Rob asks with a slow grin.

"Well, that, yes, but also when she's from." I wait for it to hit him.

Rob's brow furrows. "You mean where she's from?"

I shake my head with slow precision. "When."

He blinks in confusion. "What?"

I lean close regardless of the fact we're the only two people in the room and keep my voice low. "She thinks she's from the year 2020."

Rob's jaw drops. "Maybe the whack on the head did more damage than I thought? We should definitely get her in for an evaluation."

"That's what I said to her." I gesture wildly. "She stormed into the bedroom. I tried calling you, but you were with a patient. Then when she came out, she was determined to leave. I tried to stop her." Helplessly, I point at my swollen nose. "She gave me a broken nose and bruised…ego before storming out." I clear my throat.

"Where did she go?"

"I don't know." I hiss when I shift the icepack to the other side. "I called Marcy before I left and told her to keep an eye out for her. I told her to call everyone at the office and have let me know if she contacts them."

"Good idea. She's got nowhere to go, so she may reach out for help."

"I hope so." The thought of Kate out in the city alone with no direction and no support stirs guilt and regret in my gut. "I should have…I don't know, done something different. I mean what the hell am I supposed to say to someone when they tell me they're from the future?"

"Your reaction is normal." Rob grabs his notepad and scribbles a number down. "Did she seem lucid when she told you?"

"Yes." I sigh. "I mean, the way she said it, I could tell she believed every word."

"Hmmm." Rob ponders this for a moment. "The day you found her, did she have anything on her that would give you any indication as to where she was from or confirm she's telling you the truth?"

I scoff. "You're not actually saying you believe her, do you?"

Rob shrugs. "There are a lot of possibilities. I'm saying maybe we should investigate a little bit more before writing it off. When we find her, we can run a scan and make sure she's physically okay." His gaze sharpens. "I've met a lot of patients with serious mental issues over the years. Kate doesn't exhibit any symptoms which cause me to think she's unstable or crazy, so to speak."

"You're right." My rational mind wars with my instincts. "I just...I need her, Rob. I feel like shit."

"I know." He pats me on the shoulder. "Go home and look through her stuff. See if you can find anything."

"She left wearing the clothes I found her in." I try to remember the morning when she was unconscious and I checked her pockets for identification. There was nothing but some garbage. "I doubt I'll find anything to help us."

"Then we need to find her." Rob hands me the paper. "This is the detective's number; in case we need to enlist some help finding her."

I slip the paper in my pocket and nod. "Thanks."

"Okay, let me clean up your nose so you can get out there and find her."

Twenty minutes later, I step out into the brisk January night. Gentle flakes of snow fall from the sky dusting my face and clothes. From here I can see the lights in the Empire State Building reflected in the falling snow. I wish Kate were here to see it. It's peaceful and beautiful. I can almost see her dancing in circles trying to catch the icy flakes on her tongue.

Shit. I need to find her. She's tainted everything, leaving impressions of herself across the city. I fucked up. I pray it's not too late.

I locate the car where Cyril is waiting and climb inside. Neither of us speak, but once we reach my building, I give him instructions to watch for her.

There's no one home when I come in the door. I half hoped she would return, or that I would find Marcy with her sitting on the couch laughing at the whole situation. But the apartment is dark and vacant of all joy.

In my room, I sort through all the clothes and makeup my sister brought. There's nothing there revealing anything of relevance. Her scent lingers in the room. My gaze fixes on the bed where I buried myself inside her and made her come with my tongue.

I shake the memories away and search the drawers beside the bed, hoping I'll find something. After a thorough search, I realize there's nothing, and if there is, she's taken it with her.

I collapse on the edge of the bed and stare out over the city. Snow cakes to the glass leaving a frosted imprint wherever there's moisture. The lights glitter beyond the pane and I'm mesmerized by the sight.

She's out there. Somewhere. I whisper a prayer for safety. Nonna used to say it at night before she went to sleep. Her way of asking for protection for those she loved. I'm not a religious person, but I can't ignore the peace it gives when I murmur the words.

My head swims, and I lie down. Her scent clings to the pillow. I slide my hand beneath it and inhale deeply careful not to bump my nose. My fingertips brush against something.

I pull a small notebook from beneath the pillow. It looks like one of mine, but when I open it, it's Kate's handwriting I see.

As I read, my jaw drops. The words are a direct portal into her thoughts. Over the past week, she's filled the pages with details and information I can't even fathom. The more I read, the more I realize how wrong I was.

Kate's not crazy. She knows things no one can possibly know. I flip through the pages, devouring the words and their implications. Then I see the papers I found in her pocket the morning we met. They're pressed flat between the pages. A ticket stub and a receipt. Nothing of consequence, until I read the dates. December 29, 2020.

Then I remember her coat. Victor's coat. No wonder it looked so familiar. It's the same coat, but hers is worn and ragged from years of use. *Holy shit.*

When the detective said there was no record of Kate, I didn't understand. But now I do.

The phone rings in the other room. Taking the notebook with me, I run to try to catch the call.

"Hello?" I pray it's Kate.

"Hey. I found her. She was at Victor's place." Marcy's voice cuts through the line.

"Was?" My heart sinks.

"Yeah. She bolted without a word." My sister's voice cracks. "But we'll find her."

Disappointment and anger, mostly at myself, coagulate into a mass pulling me into darkness. "Shit." I throw the notebook down and it splays open on the floor. A simple, rudimentary sketch of a building lay between the creased pages. Then it hits me.

"I know where she is. I'll call you later." Without waiting for Marcy's response, I hang up the phone and snatch the book off the floor. As I dart out the door, I tuck it into my pocket and race down to the lobby.

Cyril is the best driver in the city, but I feel I could have made better time on foot. We're stuck in a traffic jam two blocks away, so I climb from the car.

"Go get her, boss." He shouts before the door slams.

I take off down the street shoving through anyone crazy enough to be out in this cold snowy night. When I reach the building, I wave to the night guards and punch the number for the observation deck.

Excitement builds inside me. She has to be here. It's the only possible place she could be. The elevator reaches the main deck, and I step out, anticipation thrumming through my veins.

I round the corner and see her standing against the railing.

The snow falling around her creates a beautiful ethereal halo of light against the dark sky.

Careful not to startle her, I step forward and call her name. "Kate."

She turns, and the last remaining hesitation falls away. I may not understand why she's here or how, but it doesn't matter. I love her and nothing can change that.

CHAPTER TWENTY-THREE
KATHERINE

I sense his presence. The snow creates a globe of silence encasing the observation deck. When he speaks my name, it's almost as if he's standing beside me whispering in my ear.

Apprehension coils around my heart protecting it. Coming here was selfish on my part. This is my spot. Dad's spot. But now I know for certain, this is Arthur's spot too. His love for this building is obvious. Perhaps that's why I followed my heart when it led me here because I knew he would find me.

I turn and gasp at the sight of the bandage across his nose highlighted by the darkening bruises. He shortens the gap between us, and I reach out to gently brush the skin of his cheek below the bandage.

"I'm sorry, Arthur." My apology is sincere, but the guilt lingers. "I didn't mean to hurt you."

"It will heal." His sad smile makes my heart ache. "Rob took care of it. Says it'll be as good as it was before it was broken."

"Oh, God." I hang my head. "I broke it? I'm so sorry. I reacted on instinct."

"Kate, it's okay." He tips my chin up. "I was worried about you."

I tense at his touch unsure if this is a trap or if he's sincere. "Because I'm crazy?"

He drops his hands and tucks them in his pockets but maintains our close proximity. "I didn't say you were crazy."

"You didn't have to say it." I exhale and a plume of steam engulfs us. "Don't you think I know how insane my story sounds? Why do you think I lied? I had to. No one would believe me." Tears sting my eyes. "I don't belong here."

"Do you want to go back?"

The question stops me, and I search his face for any signs

of duplicity. I find only sincerity in the depths of his gaze. "No. Everyone I love is gone. They're all here." I laugh at how stupid it sounds. "But I'm not part of this world. I haven't even been born yet. I'm a random piece of a second-hand puzzle that got tossed in the wrong box. I want to belong, but I don't know how it would even be feasible."

"There must be a reason this happened."

"When you figure it out, let me know." I scoff and narrow my gaze. "Are you saying you believe me?"

"The world is full of endless possibilities." He shrugs one shoulder. "Who am I to question the will of the universe when it drops a beautiful and talented woman right on my doorstep?"

"You make me sound like I'm special." I tease him, but his words ignite an ember of hope deep in my soul.

"You are special, Kate." He brushes a snow crusted curl away from my face. "In two weeks, you've upended my life in the best way, and I was stupid to fight it. You challenge me and make me want to be better. I can't imagine going forward without you by my side."

His touch warms me and the ember sparks into a flame.

"I apologize for my reaction earlier, and if you'd rather stay with your parents..." He pauses as though still coming to terms with the concept of Victor and Nora being my parents, but pushes forward. "Then it's fine with me. I'll even help you find your own place, if you want to take things slow."

"Thank you." I cup his hand against my cheek.

"I love you, Kate."

His confession steals my breath.

"I love you, and I don't care if you came from another planet, let alone another millennium, I want you by my side from this moment forward." Snow nearly covers his hair making him look like a sexy silver fox. His eyes shine with hope and desire.

I can't imagine any place I'd rather be than right here, right now.

"When I found you, I had no idea what to expect. Last week, the thought terrified me, but as long as I have you, I'm ready for whatever challenge lies ahead."

"Even if I refuse to give any spoilers for the future?" I grin.

"Keep all your spoilers, Kate." He hugs me tight. "All I want is you."

"I love you, Arthur." I grasp his coat in both hands and pull him closer. He kisses me, and I melt against him.

The kiss turns passionate and I brush the tip of his nose with mine. He hisses in a breath.

"Oh, I'm sorry." I wince. "Maybe we should take it easy until you recover."

"Wherever you learned that self-defense trick, it's definitely effective."

I grin and think of the first time I tried it on my ex after I watched *Miss Congeniality*. Poor bastard ended up with two black eyes, and we didn't have sex for a month afterward. It should have been a warning sign. I shove the memory to the trash bin in my head.

My past doesn't matter, because now I have a clean slate. It's a do-over in a way, and my heart feels lighter than it has in years.

"Shall we go home?" Arthur offers his arm.

I loop mine through and lean against him. "Yes. As much as I'm enjoying this *Sleepless in Seattle* moment, my toes are frozen."

Arthur shakes his head. "I have no idea what that means."

We head for the elevator, and I tug on his arm. "Spoilers without context. You'll figure it out one day." I chuckle. "This is going to be more fun than I thought."

"I'm glad you're amused, sweetheart."

Inside the elevator we dust each other off leaving a layer of snow on the carpet. Mike, the guard, waves when we exit the building, unconcerned with our presence in his building.

Cyril grins when he sees us. "I'm glad you're safe, ma'am."

"Kate." I return his infectious grin. "Call me Kate."

He nods and opens the door. Once we're in the car, Arthur pulls me against him and kisses my cheek.

"Will you stay with me?" he whispers hot against my ear.

I suppress a shiver of need and nod. "I'll stay."

"Are you going to tell your parents?" His voice is low.

"No. I don't think that's a good idea." I sigh at the thought. "It's better this way."

"I agree." He brushes my hair away from my face and smiles. "But you can spend as much time with them as you want."

"That sounds like the perfect plan." I'm blindsided by a thought and it makes me hesitate. "But what about me? I mean, not this me, baby me?"

He ponders this for a moment. "I don't know. I guess we'll address that once you're born."

"Do you think the universe will implode if I meet my infant self?" My mind spins with insane possibilities.

"I doubt it." He interlaces his fingers with mine. "Don't worry. We'll figure this out together."

"I know." I rest my head against his shoulder and close my eyes. After a few breaths, my body relaxes and peace settles over the chaos in my mind. "How did you know where to find me?"

"Educated guess." He shifts and pulls something from his pocket. "I saw your sketch in here."

Straightening, I take the notebook from his hand and hold it against my chest. "You read it?"

"I did."

"Arthur! Spoilers." Panic starts to rise once more.

"I highly doubt the universe will implode if I know a few details about the future." He chuckles. "If I wasn't financially secure, I would say there are a few prime opportunities one could take advantage of."

"You can't. It wouldn't be right." I clutch the notebook tighter.

"Don't worry, sweetheart. I'm perfectly capable of managing my wealth without the aid of insider information." He winks. "As for some of the other events you discuss, well, I doubt anyone would believe us even if we tried to warn them of impending destruction."

"You're probably right." I tap the notebook and ease my grip a fraction. "Is this why you came after me? I mean, after reading it, you must have realized I wasn't crazy or you would have called the cops."

"I came after you because I love you and I wanted to ensure your safety." He kisses my forehead. "But yes, the *spoilers* in your little journal helped solidify my belief in your story."

"I should burn this damn thing."

"If that's what you wish."

The rest of the drive is silent. A gentle contentment settles around us once we arrive home.

Home. It's so strange to think of it as my home.

I glance up at the massive building and then at the man standing tall beside me. He takes my hand and squeezes infusing me with confidence. The snow falls around us gently enfolding us in snapshot of picture-perfect winter magic.

I may not understand how I became stranded in 1985, but I understand the reason I'm meant to stay. Arthur, my dad's boss, and the man I love beyond reason. Beyond time itself.

CHAPTER TWENTY-FOUR
ARTHUR

New Year's Eve, 2020

Spoilers. Such a simple, inconspicuous word, and yet for the last thirty-five years, it has been our secret code for knowing the unknowable.

"Did you fall asleep already?" Kate calls from the doorway.

"How can anyone sleep with you nagging them to death?" I snap back in a loving tone.

"For that comment, I'm drinking both these hot cocoas." She ambles into the room with a tray bearing cookies and two steaming mugs.

Her hair, as well as mine, turned white years ago. She may have a strange little shuffle when she walks and her face is careworn with the passage of time, but she's still the same beautiful woman I married in 1985.

"Are we watching *Doctor Who* reruns?" I ask as she sets the tray down on the table.

"I was hoping we could watch *An Affair to Remember.*" She smiles. "It's a classic."

"It's better than *Sleepless in Seattle.*" I snort and reach for a cookie.

She slaps my hand. "Not better. Different. I prefer Grant to Hanks."

"You like older men," I tease her and plant a kiss on her cheek before snatching the cookie with awkward grace.

Kate sticks her tongue out and pulls her phone from her apron. "Nearly midnight, maybe we should wait for twelve and then turn in."

"You want a little New Year nookie." I add a wink, and she blushes. I love that after all these years, I can still make her blush.

"Oh, Arthur, you never change." She turns up the volume on the television and flips until a movie catches her attention.

I study her profile. She's my best friend, the love of my life, and the woman I didn't know I needed to keep me in line. How did I get so lucky?

My gaze drifts to the row of photographs lining the wall and taking up all the space on the bookshelves. Photos of us through the years, with her parents, with her holding herself as a baby, which still makes me chuckle. But the best photographs are of our kids and grandkids. My heart swells with pride at the life we created together and how amazing the journey has been.

Kate never did tell her parents. She spent as much time with them as she could up until the day her dad passed. I held her as she wept the day before and then every night for a month after. We mourned his death together. I lost my friend the day she lost her father. She never regretted stealing those final moments with him, even though he didn't know her role in his life.

When Nora and little Kate moved away, we kept in touch, but time and distance, like everything else, pushes people in different directions. We often spoke about checking on Nora and little Kate, but we knew their lives were on a set path and wanted to give them their memories together. So, we focused on our own blossoming family and left the future in the past.

Kate pulls the phone out again and glances at the time. She heaves a sigh and sips her cocoa.

"Shall we retire?" I rest my hand on her thigh.

She stares at me over her silver rimmed glasses and shakes her head. "You're still a randy old goat."

"Your magic still works on me, love." I grin, but it softens when I see the concern in her eyes. "Don't worry about her. It'll work out."

"I know." Unlocking her phone, Kate pulls up the directory. Before I can stop her, she's hit the call button.

"Kate." I reach for the phone, but she jerks it away. My voice softens. "Let it go, sweetheart."

The phone rings a few more times. Kate's eyes fill with tears.

"You already know how this story ends." I take her hand and kiss her fingertips.

She sobs and ends the call, tossing the phone aside. I gather her into my arms and hold her against me.

"I love you, Kate."

"I love you too, Arthur."

"Thanks for the memories." I kiss her tenderly. "And the spoilers."

"Let's text the kids and go to bed."

I slide my hand over her hip and squeeze her backside. "Good idea. I've got plans for you, sweetheart."

Outside in the streets, the city erupts into celebration as the new year arrives right on time.

THE END

OTHER BOOKS BY KIRSTEN S. BLACKETER

CRAVING 1985 SERIES
When I Found You
Can't Fight This Feeling
She Gives Love a Bad Name
Owner of a Lonely Heart
Just What I Needed

HISTORICAL
An Irresistible Shadow
A Shadow's Kiss
Mississippi Moonshine
Deceiving the Earl
Jewel of Winter
At Winter's Demand
Under Winter's Control
Seducing Winter's Gentleman
Stealing the Widow's Heart
Seduction on the Alpine Express
Temptation on the Alpine Express

CONTEMPORARY
A Lockdown Love Affair
A Holiday Love Affair
Mistletoe and Mistakes
Confessions of a Fangirl
Confessions of a Gamer Girl
Confessions of a Glamour Girl
The Flight Before Christmas

FANTASY/FAIRYTALE
Curse of the Huntsman's Jewel
The Huntsman's Revenge

PIRATES AND PERSUASION
Queen Takes Hook

ABOUT THE AUTHOR

Kirsten S. Blacketer is a multi-published indie author of both historical and contemporary romance. When she's not writing, she homeschools her two children and enjoys time with her family. In those moments of freedom, she devours romance novels while sipping a glass of wine. Age has only shown her that writing villains can be just as fun as heroes. Her next life goals are to write a New York Times Bestseller and one day have Adam Driver play a starring role in a film version of one of her books. A girl can dream, right?

Read more at **http://kirstensblacketer.com.**

ALSO WRITES AS JEN BRADLEE